Ollie & Joey

Go to a Café

Book 1

Alyssa Reaves

ISBN 978-1-73611-800-9

Dedicated to my mom.
I couldn't have done it without you.

Love,

Alyssa

Keep Track

School days can put you into a daze
So, grabbing your calling from a café
May be what you need to do on a rainy day.
If 1 has 2
Then, 2 has 3
For 4 to have 5
And 6 to times 3 –
You're then off to an age of higher imagination
Related to the education
You have from your foundation
A destination
Overruling societal expectation
So, start by driving and discovering together
Without hesitation
Without an ounce of fear
Choose not to allow time-consuming events
Or the loss in a sense of direction to
Interfere.
Forgive your brother for stealing your
Turkey sandwich
While it sits so far
Yet so very near.

A Turkey Sandwich ♂

"She did not!" Oliver yelled.

"She did too!" Joseph cried.

"Nope!"

"Yes!"

"Left!"

"Right!"

"Up!"

"Down!"

"Stop it — both of you! Joseph, I did not make the sandwiches differently. Now, go get that room cleaned before you leave this house." The boys' mother, Aria, gulped down her coffee while racing the clock.

"You really need to go get your eyes checked. Our sandwiches are clearly the same," Oliver said, holding up both bagged sandwiches.

"Yours smells better," Joseph whined.

"Fine, then you must —"

"I must be what?"

"You must be losing your mind!"

"Oliver, that's not nice," their dad, Justin, said. He was rubbing his eyes after having stumbled into the kitchen.

"Justin, I need you to drive the boys to school today." Aria grabbed her waterproof, black coat and searched high and low for her purse.

"Why aren't they walking with the Neighborhood School Volunteer as they usually do?" Aria stared intently at her husband and pointed out the window. He nodded at the buckets of water falling from the sky and sighed. "Alright, well, I'm going to need some coffee first."

"But you don't drink coffee," Oliver said, raising one eyebrow.

"Your dad was up all night. I wouldn't be surprised if he wanted three cups of joe," Aria laughed.

"Who is Joe?" Oliver asked.

"No one," Aria replied, sifting through her purse.

"Oh, please. I was not up all night," Justin smiled and slowly sipped his coffee.

"I just think it's all probably picking back up," Aria sighed.

"What is?" Oliver questioned.

"Nothing," Aria and Justin said simultaneously.

"Your father was just up talking." Aria turned her back to everyone and began doing various things in the kitchen.

"Mom, what did Dad say while he was sleep-talking?" Joseph asked.

"Well, whatever I said, it must have been

very important," Justin laughed before being met by their Australian shepherd, Jasper, and Toy poodle, Sapphire, who were demanding to be pet.

"Yeah, well I have no idea what you said because I was too busy trying to fall back asleep. The puppies even walked into our room to see what all your gibberish was about. I told them you were fine, so they went back to sleep."

"You should've let them investigate. Maybe they would've helped me out," Justin laughed.

"They seemed to be more thankful that I told them they didn't have to," Aria said.

"You act like you can speak to dogs," Justin laughed while rolling his eyes.

"Smart people can," Aria replied, joining him in laughter.

"You guys are embarrassing," Joseph said bluntly.

"They aren't embarrassing. They're just not funny," Oliver replied.

"I wonder how my plants are doing out there." Justin re-directed his attention out the window.

"In this weather? Good luck," Aria scoffed.

"Well, good weather or bad, it's hard to get anything to grow nowadays," Justin replied.

"Alright, well, hurry and get ready. Given all this rain, traffic probably won't be in your favor." She grabbed an umbrella after kissing the boys on the head. "Oh, Justin, the alarm has been going off on your phone. I've been snoozing it to let you sleep in a little." Justin dragged his feet to look at his phone while Aria headed out the door.

"Uh-oh." Justin's eyes grew wide.

"What?" Aria turned around.

"I forgot about this. I have an early client appointment today."

"What? You usually label those alerts!"

"I guess I forgot to."

"I wouldn't have snoozed your phone three times if I had known!" As Aria gulped down the last of her coffee, Sapphire brushed up against her ankle, and Jasper put his wet nose to her shoe. Their touches of comfort made her suddenly relax. "Alright, well, I'll ask my sister." She quickly began pressing buttons on her cell phone.

"Dad, can't we just stay here and go to work with you?" Joseph pleaded.

"No, bud — sorry. You know you can't work with me."

"Yeah, yeah. Confimintology," Joseph said, looking glumly to the floor.

"Confidentiality," Justin corrected.

"Well, Mom, can we go to work with you today?" Oliver pleaded.

"My work has similar confidentiality expectations as your father's — but, anyway, it's a school day for you, so no."

"Sitting inside your job may automatically make us smarter! Then, we can skip grades and be college graduates by the time we're thirteen or something!" Oliver exclaimed.

"Mazel tov," Aria mumbled.

"Ah, nice Hebrew — or Yiddish, rather!" Justin applauded.

"What's that? Another language?" Joseph asked.

"Oui oui," Aria replied in her best French accent. "I work with a lot of people from a number of different backgrounds, so I pick up on the languages they know or learn after having vacationed somewhere. I never take the time off work that most people do to travel and learn it first-hand."

"Aria, I keep telling you that you should," Justin replied. "No one gets an award for how much they missed out on life while they were supposed to be living it. You gotta choose to work so that you can live. Don't just live so you can work."

"So, anyway, if Oliver will be a thirteen year old college graduate, I will be fifteen!" Joseph exclaimed, ignoring his parents' off-topic discussion.

"No one would care then. It's more interesting for a thirteen year old to be a college graduate than it is for a fifteen year old to be one. Also, whenever people find out you graduated college but have the world's messiest room, they'll cancel you in a heartbeat!"

"Nuh-uh, I'll be so spectacular and rich by the time I'm a fifteen year old college graduate, I'll hire someone to always be there to clean my room!"

"Just when I thought it couldn't get any sadder," Oliver replied.

"Well, it's actually sad that you act older than me even though you're not — and since you do, people will think you're the old man graduating from college even though it'll be me!" Joseph exclaimed.

"I think you just made fun of yourself."

"Whatever, I'm older so I'm automatically smarter!"

"You have age and wisdom confused," Oliver replied.

"Alright, please maintain decency and control in your communications, boys. Your Aunt Oliva responded to me and she'll be here shortly. I'm late for being early to work — so, bye." Aria slammed the door behind her.

"Dad, you guys always say we can't go to work with you, but we know tons of kids who get to go to work with their parents and they keep confimintology — at least I think they do," Joseph said.

"Yeah, and plus, we don't even know what confimintology means so we're definitely going to keep it," Oliver added.

"Confidentiality means, well, kind of that things are top secret, like, very private," Justin said calmly as he put on his reading glasses.

"Secret?" Oliver and Joseph questioned in unison.

"Yes, so focus on the jobs you truly have."

"But, Dad, we don't have jobs," Oliver replied.

"Yes, you do. You have jobs of going to school and doing the best you can on all of your work — and you, Joseph, have the extra job of keeping that room clean."

"Yes, but we want cooler jobs than all of that," Joseph whined.

"Yeah, like saving the world!" Oliver jumped up and down.

"Well, then when you get older, you can focus on all of that." Their dad then took a seat at the kitchen table and began reading through a holiday baking magazine.

"Dad, don't you have to get ready for your appointment?" Joseph asked.

"Oh, geez, I forgot!" Justin dashed out the kitchen.

"Why does Dad forget so much?" Oliver asked.

"No clue. What did Mom mean about something picking back up with him?"

"How should I know?" Oliver asked.

"Well, all I know is I'm taking your turkey sandwich!" Joseph announced.

"No, you're not! You don't make any sense about anything!" Oliver snatched his lunch bag from Joseph's hands.

"Well, I'm older, so I don't expect you to understand any of the senses that I can and do absolutely make!"

"Why make cents when you can make dollars?" Oliver asked with a smile.

"What?" Joseph questioned.

"I don't know. I heard someone say it once." Just then, the doorbell rang, followed by a clink, a smack, and a thud noise coming from outside the front door.

"Well, I definitely have enough sense to know one thing. The person just as messy as me has arrived," Joseph smiled.

A Drive With Aunt Olivia ♋

"Dude, let me just see your sandwich." Joseph begged.

"It's sad you're still talking about this," Oliver replied.

"Just trade sandwiches with me."

"No, let it go."

"Silencio, por favor!" Aunt Olivia pleaded.

"You know Spanish?" Joseph asked.

"I've forgotten all but that sentence so hopefully it will serve its purpose right now." She sulked as she approached a stop sign. Olivia loved her nephews, and she loved spending time with them. In fact, she was always nagging her sister about never getting the opportunity to be one-on-one with them so she could fulfill her dream of being the fun aunt. However, as of today, she realized her sister had no idea what fun actually was. Her sister woke her up before it was legal to function — just so she could spend the morning in traffic during Poseidon's temper tantrum. "You know, boys, Aunt Olivia must love you because she hasn't even had her coffee yet." She peeked at the boys, then at herself through the rearview mirror. Olivia enjoys taking her time to get ready. Her style is casual-chic, but trendy — which takes time to put together. Although jumpers, rompers, and bold colored dresses fill her closet, her go-to style seems to always be blue jeans and a blazer. In whatever clothing Olivia models, she makes sure to stay true to accessorizing it. She accessorizes her neck with layered necklaces and decorates her fingers with skinny gold rings. When she feels she's having an exceptionally great hair day, she wears hoop earrings to accentuate her luscious curly brown hair. Whether she is looking at you or not, her hazel eyes seem to always smile at you. She knows how to make you laugh, and is seldom confrontational. Whenever she feels the need to be direct, she is as bold as a lion. She has a free spirited nature which helps in her relationship with God. Just like her mother, Olivia believes anyone she befriends will eventually show themselves to be much like a goose which lays no golden egg. That's why she feels a relationship with Him is safer, kinder, more patient, understanding, and trustworthy. As close as she feels to Him, Olivia believed today was a day she and God were not on the same page. She didn't understand how He would allow her to wake up to such vexing phone alerts from her sister so she could be responsible for children she personally reaped no tax benefits from. She was also baffled by His authorization of her purse turning inside out in the rain. Since she had no time to personally dry off her belongings, she delegated that task to her favorite nephews.

"Why are you and Mom so in love with coffee?" Oliver asked.

"You'll understand when you start paying bills and have a spouse who drives you crazy," Aunt Olivia replied as she brushed a fallen eyelash off her cheek.

"But, Aunt Olivia, you don't have a husband. Do you even have a boyfriend?" Joseph asked.

"Shhh!" she snapped, as she approached a red light.

"Why can't Mom ever be the one to drive us to school?" Oliver asked.

"Your mother works long hours," she said, taking a bite out of a random half eaten energy bar she found next to a random lifeguard whistle in the seat next to her. "You know, that is, whether we feel Supreme World Judges are *working* at all," she muttered in between bites as the light turned green.

"I still don't know why she can't drive us and has to work so much in secret. I mean, the taco supreme from Bell of Taco is good and the supreme pizza from Hut's Pizza is great! The world is good!" Oliver exclaimed. Aunt Olivia began laughing hysterically. Her laughter confused Oliver because he wasn't trying to be funny.

"Alright, boys, I hope you're done dabbing the rest of my things dry because here's your stop," Aunt Olivia announced as she pulled up to the front of a school. They were surrounded by mansions. Although, the area around these estates were not as picturesque as you'd imagine them to be. The sidewalks had been disturbed by unearthed tree roots and were bulging open, many plants had trouble blossoming, trees had very little leaves on them, and the facade of the school building they were parked in front of was covered in dry, brittle moss. It was as though the school building was ashamed of its community and was trying to bury itself away.

"This place looks interesting, but we don't go to school here, Aunt Olivia," Oliver said.

"What do you mean?" she asked with both shock and dismay. Joseph and Oliver looked at each other not knowing how else to explain it.

"I mean, we can try it out," Joseph shrugged while handing his aunt the various items they had dried for her. The idea of her dropping them off here sounded convenient, but she knew her sister would throw a fit if she agreed.

"No, I'll take you to the right school. With all this rain falling more and more now, you'd think your parents would glorify homeschooling so they didn't have to worry themselves or worry me about any kind of commute. Anyway, how do we get to your school?" She shifted gears from 'park' to 'drive' with a yawn.

"We don't know," Oliver shrugged.

"Well, it can't be that far since sometimes you walk," she said, trying to encourage them to think a bit harder. It was 7:40 a.m. and school started at 8:00 a.m. She had picked the boys up forty minutes ago, but didn't physically leave their house until 7:24 a.m., which means she spent sixteen minutes worth of unnecessary gas driving to the wrong school. Realizing this, she sighed aloud. "What's the name of your elementary school?" The boys looked at each other and busted out into non-stop laughter. "Why are you laughing?" she asked with subtle irritance in her tone.

"It's the same elementary you went to — like fifty years ago, right?" Joseph asked.

"Hey!" she snapped. "Much less than that, thank you very much!"

"Sorry," Joseph replied, putting his head down and yawning. Just like his aunt, he was not a morning person.

At 7:58 a.m., Joseph and Oliver arrived at their school, kissed their aunt good-bye, and sprinted to class. After Aunt Olivia watched the boys run in between the drops of rain, she turned to face the road ahead. "I need some energy — and coffee won't cut it."

"Yeah, but it seems like we've been walking for forever, so I'm pretty sure I have had a birthday by now."

"Let's make up a song — or a rap!" Joseph exclaimed, ignoring his brother's tendency to be lost and confused with time.

"OK, what do I do?"

"Drop a beat!" Joseph replied.

"Why would I drop anything in this rain right now, Joseph?"

"It's a figure of speech, Oliver. We're learning about metaphors and similes in class now."

"OK. Tell me more."

"That was it. That's how class ended. I mean, you know, Mr. Teacher —"

"Why are you calling him 'Mr. Teacher' when his name is Mr —"

"No!" Joseph exclaimed. "Mr. Teacher is his name until he has earned his title. I am careful with whom I trust, Oliver, and with that, I am careful with whom I call by full name."

"So, you call him 'Mr. Teacher' to his face?"

"No, no. I get by without calling him anything, really."

"So, what does he call you?"

"Joseph. That's what I expect. That's my name."

"So, you have him call you by your name, but you won't call him by his?"

"Don't question your elders, Oliver."

"Don't be a hippo," Oliver replied.

"You mean a hypocrite?" Joseph questioned.

"Yeah. Glad you've heard of it."

"Well, duh, — I'm older," Joseph scoffed.

"It's not about age. It's about experience. I would know, I'm the wiser one," Oliver replied.

"Are we going to rap, or what?" Joseph was eager to redirect the conversation. Oliver rolled his eyes and motioned for his brother to continue. "Well, Mr. Teacher literally explained today that we are going to learn about similes and metaphors when we get back from break. He said it right before the dismissal bell rang today. He gave us one example though. He started beatboxing — then he was like, 'You can drop a beat like a rap song, but don't drop your chili on my turkey sandwich, son.' That's a cool rap, huh?" Joseph asked with excitement.

"Oh, just beautiful — including the turkey sandwich."

"Yeah?"

"No, it's lame, Joseph." Oliver rolled his eyes. The boys continued walking while wiping raindrops off their faces. Since the wind was generously showering them with so much rain, they were quickly getting a chill. As a distraction from the cold, Joseph focused his attention on the sounds he heard around him. He listened to the cars rushing through puddles, rain droplets dripping off tree leaves, and the sound of his and Ollie's feet dragging along the sidewalk. When the rain decided to let up some, Joseph began beatboxing.

"OK, now you gotta drop a beat, Oliver," Joseph insisted.

"I'm not dropping anything — and why is it called beetbox? Beets are gross."

"It's not beets, the vegetable. It's beats — like a rhythm of music you make with your mouth." Just then, Joseph lost his balance and fell to the ground.

"Looks like you just dropped the beats for the both of us," Oliver laughed as he helped his brother up. While the rain took a recess, Oliver took the opportunity to scan his surroundings. "Should we take a break at that café over there?" He pointed to a rather large café in the distance. "Mom took us there before, so I don't think we're far from home." Sniffing back tears from the pain he felt from his fall, Joseph nodded in agreement. He focused on the café in the distance. The red, orange, and blue colors on it were magnetic.

It took about one-hundred more steps for the boys to arrive in front of the café. They sat under its pergola that had a cover over it so no raindrops could fall through. Joseph was still whimpering. The rain must have become annoyed with his moaning because another downpour began. As they peered through the windows of the café, they found it to be quite a popular place. People of all ages were taking time to enjoy the café's energy. Customers were enjoying slices of cake, unique croissants, and a variety of coffees and teas. The walls were beige and dark red. The fireplaces must have done their jobs because some customers even had their coats hanging on the backs of their chairs. Everyone inside seemed content as they stirred their drinks and ate their pastries while laughing at one another's jokes. Though Oliver and Joseph weren't partaking in this direct joy, they were enjoying no longer being hit in the face with water.

"Should we drop a beat?" Oliver asked, breaking the silence and hoping to cheer his brother up who was now examining the scrape he had on his elbow.

"Go ahead," Joseph responded without eye contact.

"Well, I don't know how to drop it," Oliver replied.

"Me neither," Joseph shrugged.

"Well, when you fell, you made a huge noise — so you *do* know how," Oliver laughed.

"Yeah!" Joseph smiled, replaying the fall in his head, finding it funnier now than ever. "BOOM! Fell flat on my face. BOOM! It was a disgrace. BUR! It's cold out here. Ohhh, I need a root beer!" Joseph exclaimed while bouncing his head to the beat of his own words.

"Wow. That was terrible. Let me try."

"Go for it," Joseph replied.

"Your stomach made a pound when it hit the ground. Thank God I came around and —"

"Boys, what are you doing out here?" A clean-shaven, tall man who appeared to be in his mid-seventies stood before them. He had a bit of a stomach, a head of thin white hair, and a plus sign tattoo on his left arm. The white apron he wore matched the bit of hair he had left on his head. The man was holding two trash bags while standing in the café's doorway. "Are your parents here?" he asked looking around.

"Hi, sir. My brother and I had to walk home from school today because Aunt Olivia forgot to pick us up — and we wanted to get home before Mom found out she forgot about us. Then, we needed a place to rest after I fell. So, please don't call the cops or tell Mom," Joseph pleaded.

"What in the world? Come inside where it's warm." The man motioned for them to enter through the café's doorway. "I have a couple of blankets I bought for my grandson, but looks like you two need them more." He set the bags of trash off to the side of the double doors. "My name is Mr. Cowfinaé."

"Thanks, Mr. Café," Joseph said quickly, grabbing his brother's hand and hurrying them inside. The man laughed at his new name and closed the door behind them.

"Why don't you two sit at that open table

underneath one of my many cake paintings? Those bags there on the table are the blankets," he said, pointing across the way. "I'll go wash up and make you boys some hot cocoa. Also, while you're sitting near the dessert case, think about what you want to eat from it. I'll be back in a jiffy to take your orders." When the man was out of sight, Oliver froze as solid as ice.

"Uh-oh," Oliver said rather loudly.

"What?" Joseph whispered. "And lower your voice."

"I can't lower my voice, Joseph. My voice is inside of my body. I am not a remote control.".

"Well, you just did it!" Joseph replied.

"Did what?"

"Never mind!" Joseph said with a bit more volume in his own speech now. "Why did you say 'uh-oh' just now?"

"Well, I think we walked so far, we're in Heaven — and we left Mom and everyone!" Ollie yelped. His brother ignored him and picked up one of the blankets.

"Don't worry, young one. We just met an angel at a café. You even said you knew this place. You said Mom took us here before, remember?" Oliver nodded at his brother's more sensible thought and undid the folds of his blanket, wrapping it around himself. The blankets were very warm after having absorbed some heat from the nearby wall-vent.

"Wow," Joseph said, redirecting both of their attentions to the dessert case. "What pastry do you want?" The boys' eyes were opened wide with excitement at the very sight of all the character cakes, intricate cupcakes, and uniquely shaped croissants they saw.

"Whatever is lowest in sugar," Oliver replied while drooling over a chocolate pistachio croissant shaped like a decadent pillow.

"You sure you aren't the older one, Oliver? You are both an old guy and a little kid in one body."

"No, Joseph. The things I say are just common sense. Too much sugar makes my head hurt so I can't stuff my mouth with too much sweet stuff." The boys continued staring at the items in the large dessert case. This dessert wall was a child's dream. It was a whole wall dedicated to proving how many different desserts existed in the world. All the basic desserts were there, such as cherry pie, sweet potato pie, carrot cake, yellow cake with chocolate icing, banana pudding, and blackberry cobbler. There were cakes in the shape of animals, soufflé's that looked like hats, and pies sculpted like childhood board games. On the dessert case was a sign that read, *Each one individually made to help your day.*

"I think I'll go with the banana pudding," Oliver said.

"Yeah. Grandma Edna used to always make that for us," Joseph smiled.

"I think you should get it too!" Oliver exclaimed.

"No, I'll get a sundae and we can split both!"

"A sundae?" Oliver questioned. Joseph pointed over to the side where a 3-flavor soft serve machine stood showcasing caramel, vanilla, and fudge flavors. The sign read, *All sundaes come with all toppings. Notify your server if you want any amendments, even though we do not recommend your amendments.* The boys read the sign in silence. "What flavor are you going to get then?" Oliver asked.

"Definitely caramel," Joseph said.

"Really?"

"Yeah. What's wrong with caramel? I mean, when's the last time you've had caramel ice cream?"

"Good point," Oliver replied.

"Mr. Café's coming!" Joseph sprinted to his chair. As Mr. Café approached, he carried two steaming cups of hot cocoa on a tray. The cups were made of pure chocolate so they would be able to eat the cups after finishing their drinks. Mr. Café placed the edible mugs in front of them and smiled. "Despite these here being two treats in one, tell me what else it'll be?"

"Thanks, Mr. Café," Joseph said, no longer feeling how cold and damp he was. "May I have a caramel sundae?"

"A sundae!" Mr. Café exclaimed. "And here I was thinking you boys were freezing — but I digress

— absolutely you may." He turned to Oliver, "And you?" As Oliver was about to announce his decision, a woman screamed from across the way. The boys turned and saw who they never imagined they would. They saw their mother.

"My babies!" she yelled, dropping her cup of coffee, almost scolding the man and woman standing near her. She ran to Joseph and Oliver so fast, you would have thought she teleported. After giving them a few kisses, hugs, and tears, she began her line of questioning. "Why aren't you with Aunt Olivia? How did you get here? Are you OK? What is going on?"

"We're fine, Mom. We're in the middle of ordering," Joseph said.

"What?" She raised one eyebrow.

"We stopped here and met Mr. Café," Joseph explained. She looked up at Mr. Café.

"I'm so sorry. I —" she began.

"Don't even mention it, Ma'am. I thought these two fine gentlemen might want to start the holidays off with my grandmother's chocolate mug hot cocoa. It's my special from now into the new year." He pointed to a flashing sign that was advertising it near the doorway.

"My sister was supposed to pick them up. I've been at work since forever, and I'm only now drinking my second cup of coffee for the day! I'm glad the coffee machine at work broke and I'm glad I decided to come here to have my second cup or…" her voice drifted.

"Don't mention it."

"I will never trust my sister again," she snarled under her breath. "Mr…" she began, but was unsure of his last name.

"Well, your boys actually gave me a fun, new name: Mr. Café. It has a nice ring to it. I might dedicate a menu item to it," he laughed.

"Mr. Café, charge me for four of those hot cocoas — but don't worry about making them. I'm also giving you something for the inconvenience my sons caused, as well as for these blankets I'm assuming you lent them." She reached inside her purse to retrieve her wallet.

"You'll do nothing of the sort," Mr. Café said sternly, holding up one hand.

"But you…" her voice drifted.

"I'll whip up another coffee for you. Just make sure your boys keep those blankets for a warm drive home. Give me a second and then you can be on your way." Before she could say anything more, Mr. Café was out of sight.

"Sorry about the spill!" she called after him, but he was too far gone. Suddenly, she turned tomato-red, scrunched her nose, pursed her lips, and yanked out her phone. She motioned for the boys to remain seated while she walked over to the other side of the café where there was only a bin full of wet umbrellas.

"$2 says Mom's yelling at Aunt Olivia," Joseph smirked.

"Joseph, money can't talk," Oliver replied.

"Hey, do you hear jazz music playing?"

"No, but it's too loud to hear music in here anyway — but speaking of jazz, did you know it started in the late 19th century and into the 20th century?"

"No. How do you know that?" Joseph asked.

"How do you not know?" Oliver questioned back.

When Mr. Café saw the boys' mother on her phone across the way, he placed her re-made cup of coffee in the middle of their table and handed them both brown paper bags.

"I put goodies inside of these to help easily transport some treats I hope you'll enjoy."

"What's transport mean?" Oliver asked.

"It means to move from one place to another," Joseph explained.

"That's right," Mr. Café said. "Now, I must get back to work. I have Thanksgiving off, but not the day after — oh, but I didn't catch your names."

"I'm Oliver."

"I'm Joseph."

"Ollie and Joey," he said with a smile.

"Wow, no one's ever called us that before," Joseph said, thinking hard.

"Well, it's only right I give you your nicknames since you gave me mine," Mr. Café smiled.

"But neither of our names are Nick," Oliver said, completely puzzled.

"Oh, and take care of those blankets. The more you do, the more they will take care of you," he said. Oliver and Joseph directed their attention to the plush royal blue blankets that were now sliding off the backs of their chairs. When they turned back around to face Mr. Café, he was nowhere in sight. So, the boys redirected their attention to observing the people around them while enjoying the warmth from the nearby fireplace. It was now raining so hard conversations from the loudest table of people closest to them couldn't be heard. When their mother finally returned to their table, her face was less red. She picked up the cup of coffee, took a big sip, and sighed.

"C'mon, boys. You'll be coming to work with me today after all."

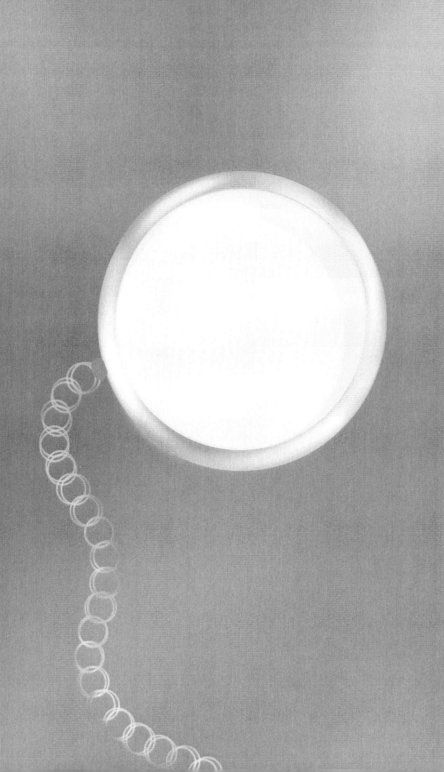

A Dream Job ♂

Oliver and Joseph had only been as far as the dull-colored lobby walls of their mother's office building. Given the break-room's basic kitchenette, table, mirror, and TV instantly greeting them, their excitement to be inside their mother's place of employment quickly subsided. The boys were very tired from their earlier walk. They had no desire to find the remote for the powered off television either. Instead, they remained sulking at the fact that the place responsible for judging supreme tacos, pizzas, and probably even nachos all day was anything but exciting and delicious. The only thing that distracted them from this revelation was the aroma of freshly printed paper filling the air from the other side of the door. The most interesting thing for them to listen to was the sound of workers rushing by, hoping to make their last minute deadlines. Nevertheless, the boys were happy to finally reach their goal of being at work with one of their parents. They were even happier to learn that the building had heat to keep them warm just like the café did.

"I think I'm going to start calling you 'Ollie' — just keep note of that," Joseph announced, abruptly breaking their silence.

"Do whatever you want," Ollie sighed as he repositioned himself as comfortably as he could in his chair.

"And you'll call me 'Joey,' right?"

"Fine, Joey!" Ollie snapped.

"Hey, no need to snap at me!"

"Sorry." Ollie pulled his blanket tighter around his shoulders. "I'm just hungry and tired."

"Well, you've been staring at that bag from Mr. Café, so go ahead and open it! Then, you can sleep on a full stomach."

"Well, I've mainly been staring at the inside of my eyelids, but whatever, maybe I will."

"Just open it."

"It's just gonna be some dessert. I'm hungry for real food, Joey!"

"Beggars can't be choosers, Ollie!"

"Well, you begged for something that Mr. Café wasn't even offering us. You begged him for ice cream when there was a whole wall of desserts in front of you!"

"It was more of a request than a beg," Joey explained calmly.

"Says you," Ollie scoffed.

"Hey, let it be known that since I am older Mr. Café and I are automatically closer in age, and therefore, have a grown up understanding of life and of the hidden meanings to things — such as, placing a simple order! I've been through a lot in my life, you know? Mr. Café understands that. That is why he allowed me to place the order I needed for my own self-care."

"OK, you have not been through a lot. The only thing you have been through is a mountain of mess — mess you chose to create inside your own bedroom," Ollie replied.

"I digest," Joey said, peacefully raising his hand.

"What are you digesting? You haven't even eaten anything yet."

"I don't know. I hear Dad say it to Mom whenever they're about to start arguing. OK, but whatever. Let's see what's inside these bags!" As the boys began opening their bags, the rain continued crying. "Hey! Trade with me!" Joey yelled at a level that competed with the rain's shrill.

"You know, you really need some help. You become irrational whenever it rains," Ollie snarled.

"Oh, big word for a six year old — irrational," Joey taunted.

"Yes, irrational — and you also become irritating!"

"Spell irrational!" Joey screamed.

"I - R- R- I don't have to!" Ollie yelled back.

"Fine. $5 says you can't spell 'irritating' either!"

"I already told you, money can't talk so it can't *say* anything!" Ollie exclaimed.

"Boys!" their mother hissed, swinging the door open and offering additional fluorescent lighting into the dimly lit room. "What are the two things you are to maintain?"

"Decency and control," the boys said simultaneously as they looked down at the carpet.

"That's right — and that applies to all of your thoughts and actions." She brushed off a piece of lent that had fallen onto her trousers. "How are you going to be successful teenage college graduates if you can't maintain decency and control? Now, your father will get here in an hour. He has to finish up with his last patient of the day. It's Ms. Patty so…" her voice drifted as she closed the door.

"Oh my gosh — not Ms. Patty!" Ollie whined. "She has Dad working for forever! I am definitely going to have a birthday and be old by the time he gets here!" Even though Joey empathized with his brother, he ignored his whining and focused on opening his bag. Inside, Joey found a blue notebook with *Left-handed+* written across it. Surprised by his brother not pulling out a dessert, Ollie reached inside his bag to discover a pair of black socks with one thin red line and one thin purple line on it. "I don't understand," Ollie said, holding up the socks.

"This is dumb," Joey said as he showed Ollie a sandwich bag with two green bone-shaped dog treats inside. What Joey didn't want to admit was that the color of the treats triggered a memory for him. It reminded him of the tall, green trees in the woods he and his father had seen a great deal of during a trip they had taken together. The trip to the woods was very far from where they lived. Joey remembered appreciating having been able to hear sounds that weren't those of the city. In addition to the green trees, the grass was the greenest green he had ever seen. He remembered all the activities they did across it. They fished, danced with animals, built a tent, and made s'mores. Ollie was much too young to go, and their mother made it clear she wanted to spend that week off from work completely indoors where there was plumbing. Joey was deep in thought reminiscing all of this, when suddenly, he became distracted by the sound of Ollie fishing for items inside of his bag. He was amazed at Ollie having pulled out a watch. It was a simple watch with a square face that simply showed the time. A folded up piece of paper was stuck to it that read, *You will figure out how to properly work this when you are ready.* "And how dumb is that note?" Joey snarled after reading it over Ollie's shoulder.

"Yeah, I don't know what this is supposed to mean — but anyway, I'm hungry," Ollie sighed, dropping the note back inside the bag.

"I know, I know. Oh, wait! Check this out!" Joey tried on a pair of sunglasses he found inside of his bag.

"Take those off. You're not cool," Ollie said.

"Whatever. This is all lame." As Joey placed the sunglasses back inside the bag, he furrowed his brow. "Uh. Why didn't I see this thing in the first place?" Joey pulled out a transparent container holding the most decadent caramel cupcake he had ever seen. It's caramel drizzle had specks of red throughout it. He couldn't explain why, but the color red always reminded him of the number three. Making connections like this was the way Joey understood things. He correlated colors with numbers, numbers with memories, memories with sounds, and so many other combinations of each. Out of fear his teachers and parents would think less of him, Joey kept his interpretation of things a secret. Now, holding the sweetest smelling cupcake in the world, Joey couldn't help but smile at the senses the smell encouraged him to embrace. He began remembering the time he ordered a dessert bigger than his head at a family dinner outing. Joey began thinking more critically about how well connected the memories and experiences he had were to one another. As Joey observed the cupcake closer, he looked at the color red circulating around it, and at the same time, saw absolutely nothing at all. Joey had grown to teach himself to watch whatever was in front of him instead of notice what was before him. A couple of years ago, Joey tried confiding with his best friend regarding the way he comprehended senses. He asked her if she knew what the color purple felt and smelled like —

hoping her answer would be somewhat similar to his. Instead, she teased him about his perception not making any sense. Since then, Joey worked hard to utilize his senses in the way he was taught to.

"Why are you staring so hard at that cupcake?" Ollie asked, causing Joey to snap out of his daze.

"What? Um, nothing." Joey quickly bit into the cupcake. "I just think it's strange I didn't see this cupcake in my bag before." Ollie looked into his bag and pulled out a seven layered banana pudding dessert.

"Woah, yeah, me too! How did I not see this before? What's this label mean?"

"Hmm, it says 'Lactose-free' but I don't know what that means. We'll have to ask Mom." The boys quickly turned their bags upside down to ensure nothing else was inside. When they confirmed both bags were completely empty, they devoured their treats. Then, Joey let out a big burp. Ollie laughed and burped back. They began having a burping contest until they ended up burping themselves to sleep.

Ollie fell asleep first and began dreaming. He appeared to be the age he was now, but everything around him was different. Men wore funny clothes and women wore even funnier ones. Most men had a top hat covering their heads, and walked with a cane for show or out of need. Some men even decorated their faces with monocles. Women wore dresses so long and poofy, you could hardly see what shoes they had on — or if they were even wearing shoes. Many women enhanced their outfits by placing shawls over their outer coats — which only highlighted their up-do hairstyles that looked like it took them hours to create.

"Why do you look lost, boy?" a tan, thin man in an all-white suit, wearing a gold tie, and gold monocle asked him. Before Ollie could speak, the man pointed across the dirt road. "Go on up those stairs." He pointed to a large building that had even larger stairs attached to it. Ollie nodded and went up the stairs. As he walked up, he saw a woman who looked very familiar. He couldn't recall who she was but her curly hair, brown skin, and captivating eyes reminded him of someone. He didn't want her to catch him staring, so he tried to listen in on what she was saying without any eye contact. She was speaking to a woman beside her.

"I don't know. I'm just so over wearing this. I want to get dressed in the morning and not spend time wondering if my bonnet matches my corset that I had to squeeze into. Don't get me wrong, I want to be fashionable, but I want it to be on my own terms."

"You know you're whining about the wrong things in life," the woman next to her replied.

"I know. It's a lost cause," she sighed. "Anyway, did you bring the green coffee beans?" The chatter from others walking the stairs instantly grew, so Ollie could no longer hear nor see either of the women. He continued up the steps before entering the building's main doorway. Inside, he saw a hallway with several home units on either side.

"This is obviously an apartment building," he thought to himself. Ollie began walking down the hallway rather confidently, somehow knowing exactly which unit to enter into.

"Oliver!" Ollie heard a voice call out to him. "Oliver!" the voice yelled louder. "Ollie!" another voice exclaimed at a much higher pitch. Suddenly, Ollie woke up inside the break-room of his mother's job with his brother and father hovering over him. Ollie realized he had fallen asleep after eating his banana pudding. He licked the corners of his mouth in hopes the sugar would help keep him alert. His father was smiling, but had a definite expression of worry on his face.

"Are you OK? We've been trying to get you to wake up for a couple of minutes now," his dad said.

"Yeah, I even burped in your face," Joey added.

"OK then when you go to sleep tonight, I'm going to burp in your face!" Ollie replied.

"I'd like to see you try."

"You won't see me try. You'll be too busy being asleep!" Ollie laughed.

"And you'll be too busy being a joke!" Joey cried.

"Guys, that's enough," their father said. "And if we can have a quiet car ride home, I'd be forever grateful. I've had enough chatter for the day. I need peace and harmony, just like my great grandmother would always say."

"Yes, Dad," the boys said in unison.

"I'm serious," their father said sternly.

"Honestly, Dad, we've had an exhausting day ourselves," Joey sighed. Ollie began gathering his things to meet his father and brother who were now standing and waiting for him at the door.

"Hey, Ollie, you dropped that," Joey said, pointing and walking over to a linked chain with a shiny, circle connected to its end. "Did this come out of the bag from Mr.Café too?"

"I don't think so," Ollie said, examining it from his brother's hand.

"What is it?" Joey held it up higher for their father to see.

"Well," their dad began, "It's a monocle."

47

A Dinner to Remember ∞

"So, let me get this straight, 'Mr. Café ' is his actual name?" their dad laughed as he drove along the wet, traffic-filled road. The boys had just finished telling him about their day — including the odd presents they found in their to-go dessert bags from Mr. Café.

"I, for one, think it's a great name or at least a great nickname," Joey announced.

"Even though his name is not Nick," Ollie added, holding his index finger high.

"But that still doesn't explain why you have a monocle, Oliver," their dad said, driving through their home community gates. "Those things are extremely rare. They haven't been popular since, well, the 19th century!"

"We can go back to Mr.Café and ask about it," Joey suggested.

"No, we do not have the time," their father replied.

"Yes, we do, Dad. Don't worry. I have a watch." Ollie struggled to show his dad the watch from the backseat.

"That's not what I meant. I refuse to be out in this rain any longer. Anyway, you said that monocle wasn't in either of the bags Mr. Café gave you, right?" The boys remained silent, understanding their dad's rhetorical point. "I mean, the monocle could have dropped out of one of your bags, or it could have been dropped by someone else who works in the building with Mom. So, I think you should return it back there."

"Dad, there wasn't much of anything in that small room when we got there. I'd like to believe I did a good scan, and everything on the ground was clean," Joey announced.

"Fine, son, then you must have just scanned over it — but tell me, while you were taking the time to scan the grounds of that room, were you not inspired to scan and clean the grounds of your own?" Everyone was silent. They let the rain's pitter-patter on the rooftop of the car do the rest of the talking. "Ugh, I need to get dinner ready before I fool around and forget." Their dad let out a deep sigh and clicked the remote control to open their garage door.

From the door to the house, the boys dashed inside to greet their dogs. Sapphire's seven pounds of wavy, beige fur and Jasper's fifty pounds of straight, reddish-brown fur were showstoppers amongst any crowd. They have similar work ethic when it comes to protecting the family, but contrasting personalities on a daily basis. Sapphire enjoys jumping and curling up in your lap as much as she enjoys being your sous-chef in the kitchen whenever you are cooking. Jasper enjoys hugging, dancing, and running you around the yard to keep your heart pumping.

"You should give the dog treats to them," Ollie said, huffing and puffing after playing with the dogs. Joey nodded and took the treats from out of his bag. Sapphire and Jasper immediately gobbled them up and began licking their lips. Whenever food was offered, these two left no crumbs behind.

"Man, they ate that so fast!" Joey exclaimed.

"Look! They're walking all over our blankets we got from Mr. Café!"

"They are always taking over any blanket they find," Joey laughed.

"How did Mr. Café even know we had dogs?" Ollie asked.

"We must sound like dog owners," Joey shrugged.

"Sound? Well, as long as I don't smell like it, I'm good."

"Boys, dinner's ready!" their dad called from afar. The boys couldn't believe dinner was ready. Despite working from home, their father tended to forget to do things he needed to do around the house. Mainly, he forgot to make dinner. Sometimes, he forgot while in the process of making it.

"Wow, this looks so good," Ollie said, staring at the steaming plate in front of him.

"I call it 'The Sapphire' since she was in here watching me cook it the first time I ever did." Sapphire stuck her tongue out, trying to taste the food by its alluring aroma. Jasper sat in his crate, biting on his chew toy. He wasn't much of a beggar, but if you chose to walk over to him and put a treat inside his bowl, he was grateful.

"So, how was Ms. Patty, Dad?" Joey asked, slurping up pasta after having maneuvered it onto his fork.

"She wasn't here as long as you'd think," he replied, chewing on a few cubes of steak before tasting the fettuccine on his plate. "How do you like the steak?"

"Good," Ollie replied, already eating his final piece. "But what does she have to talk so much about?" Ollie said while twirling noodles onto his fork.

"I help people through stresses they have in life. When they need to talk about something sad or confusing that happened to them, I help guide —"

"Yeah," Ollie interrupted, "But what all does she spend time saying to you?"

"You know I can't discuss that," he replied.

"It's confimintology," Joey said proudly.

"Confidentiality," their dad corrected while

52

laughing.

"That's what I said," Joey said, joining him in laughter before drinking his ice water in front of him. Joey loved water with ice. The fact water could be inside of water fascinated him. Chewing ice or listening to it clink against a glass was a calming sound to him.

"You and Mom both have jobs where you keep secrets," Oliver whined.

"Buddy, we talked about this, but you'll understand when you're...taller."

"Well, I actually grew an inch yesterday!" Ollie said with excitement.

"No, you didn't," Joey said as he got up to place his empty plate and glass inside the kitchen sink.

"You eat as fast as Jasper and Sapphire — but anyway, yes I did so grow taller!"

"You don't even know what an inch is!"

"You don't even know your face!" Ollie screamed.

"Boys!" their Mom snapped as she walked into the kitchen. No matter how long of a work day she had or how stressed out she was, Aria's outfits kept her looking lively. Her professional wardrobe consisted of conservative items that had fashionable style to them. Any hint of bags under her eyes never fully presented themselves on her face either. Even if they had, you'd be delightfully distracted by the coat she purposely matched to her shoes or belt. "I take you to work, and hear you yelling. I come home — more yelling?" She turned to her husband, "Justin, why didn't you..."

"They just..." Justin began, trying to defend himself, but then decided diverting the conversation would be best. "How was work, Aria?" He got up from his chair and helped her remove her coat.

"It's over," she said, walking over to the kitchen table where a plate was waiting for her. "And I took a week of vacation. I haven't taken one that long since you and Joey went on that camping trip." She took a bite of her pasta and sighed.

"Well, tomorrow we can get started on the decorations," Justin said.

"Sweetheart, we need to figure out Thanksgiving before we decorate this place for Christmas," she said, taking another bite of pasta. "My mother wants us with her for Christmas," she said, gazing down at the cubed pieces of steak on her plate. The boys' grandmother had a large heart filled with care, but it was masked with worry, fear, and a short-temper regarding almost anything. This strong personality made her unapproachable to the average person. She kept a strict household where ordinary things you were used to doing, such as turning on a kitchen faucet or cleaning up a spill, you had to relearn her way.

"Any word from Olivia?" Justin asked, finishing up the remaining noodle on his plate.

"I called her, but no answer," Aria replied, stabbing steak cubes onto her fork.

"Well, we got it figured out now so all is well," he said, pouring both Aria and himself blueberry juice in tall glasses.

"No, she is such a —" Aria began, but chose to eat more pieces of steak rather than finish her sentence. She took a sip from her glass before continuing to scoop more steak onto her fork. "I'm so exhausted. I can hardly eat. I'll save the rest for later," she said, putting her fork down before leaning back in her chair. "Come, Sapphire, let's go lay down." Justin motioned his help in putting away her leftovers while Sapphire jumped up and down next to Aria's leg as a signal of her desire to be carried. Aria picked up Sapphire, carrying her into the family room where they routinely lounged together in the large massage chair before falling asleep.

"Go shower, boys," Justin said with his back turned to them as he poured his wife's leftover juice into his glass. The boys got up from the table and headed toward their individual bathrooms.

"We should look at our gifts from Mr. Café again," Joey whispered, stopping Ollie in his tracks.

"Why are you whispering? It's not a secret," Ollie replied.

"You want me to yell and get us in trouble?"

"Why are yelling and whispering the only two options?"

"Shh, and tell me what you think happened to Aunt Olivia," Joey snapped.

"She's probably trying to get away from you — you irrational little boy who should be working on getting into college instead of playing with gifts all day!" Ollie slammed the bathroom door in his brother's face.

Later on, while in his bedroom, Joey re-played the events of the day over in his head. He thought about the beginning of the day with Aunt Olivia and her usual messy car. Then, he thought about the conversation he had with his brother during lunch at school. As he reminisced, he listened to the sounds he heard around him. He did his best to fade out the city noises of motorcycles revving up, car horns honking, and buses braking. He tried his best to focus on God's nature-made noises of leaves rustling along the ground, crickets chirping all around, and rain showering down. He listened to these nature sounds as long as he could before getting distracted by his mother who was on the phone and walking back and forth in the hallway right outside his door. Joey began to wonder if the way he interpreted sight, sound, taste, touch, and smell weren't too strange to tell others. Maybe the teasing he experienced in the past was a one time thing that he should let go. Maybe he wasn't the only one in the world who connected senses and understood things this way. As he sat up from his pillow, he saw the sunglasses from Mr. Café sitting on the edge of his dresser. Since Jasper was fast asleep on the rug below, Joey tip-toed quietly to rescue the sunglasses from their possible fall. He put them on and suddenly saw vibrant colors all around. He was amazed at how animated the colors all were. All his senses started working at once. He could taste orange, smell blue, feel green, hear yellow, and so on. Joey was in awe as much as he was petrified. When he turned around and looked back at his bed, he gasped. Jasper was sitting on his bed, staring directly at him.

"You know, I really appreciated that treat you gave me earlier," Jasper said.

"Don't mention it," Joey replied. He then gasped, realizing he had just communicated with Jasper in plain English. "Wait. What?"

"Nothing. Go back to sleep," Jasper said as he jumped back onto the rug. Joey froze in terror. Was he dreaming? How did he just speak to Jasper?

Did these sunglasses have magical powers? Was Mr. Café a real person? Was today a whole dream? He took the sunglasses off and threw them to the end of his bed where it hit against a pillow that was on its way to falling off the bed. Joey then went straight to sleep — truly feeling the exhaustion of the day.

A Gingerbread Smelling Kitchen ♂

"What are you doing?" Joey asked Ollie.

"Very busy right now," Ollie said as he organized various items in his room.

"Busy doing what?"

"A lot, Joseph."

"OK, Oliver, I know you now only call me 'Joseph' when you mean business. Also, you're six so you have no business to even....mean."

"Listen, I have six years worth of actual work to do and *you*, my friend, have eight years worth." Joey let out a deep exhale and pursed his lips at his brother continuing to tidy up miscellaneous items in his room.

"OK, Ollie, tell me what you have to do today — on Thanksgiving Day of all days!"

"My race cars need cleaning, my building blocks are missing and need finding, my dinosaurs need to eat, and all my superhero toys need to work out, OK? So, if there's not anything else, I'll see you on my lunch break — even though I don't think I will be eating because my tummy hurts from breakfast." Joey gave his brother a big look of disbelief, which caused Ollie's anger to grow. "Whatever, good-bye, Joseph!" Ollie slammed the door shut in Joey's face. Joey knew his brother complained after eating certain foods, but he never knew why. All he understood now was that Ollie wanted to be left alone, but Joey wasn't going to be considerate of that.

"Only babies get tummy aches so you need to grow up like only sometimes you know how to do! Also, all we had for breakfast was french toast and yogurt!" Joey used the silence he heard in response to his taunting as encouragement to bestow further insight. "Maybe you were battling with a ninja in your dream and ended up punching *yourself* in the stomach and that's why you have a stomachache!" Joey's snarky remark did, in fact, remind Ollie of the odd dream he had. However, there was no ninja-fighting that took place in it. Nevertheless, it was a peculiar, unsettling dream. Notably and oddly enough, his big brother's infatuation with the sound of his own voice was actually less unsettling than the gurgling noises his stomach was now making. Although, instead of wallowing about this, Ollie re-opened his door to calmly talk to Joey.

"Joey?"

"Yeah?"

"Eating food is taken for granted."

"What do you mean?" Joey raised an eyebrow.

"I mean when people with food allergies eat something that doesn't make them sick, they appreciate not being sick, right? Well, those people who get to eat all the food in the world and not get sick don't realize the superpowers they really have!"

"So, what you're saying is, I have super powers and you don't because breakfast today made you sick and not me?"

"Well, I'm starting to think a lot of food can be good or bad — even good food can be bad to some people, like, just because something is good to your body doesn't mean it'll be good to mine. Also, did you know someone is out there cloning food? I think I saw something about it on TV once. You think you went to the store and bought real chicken, real bread, or real bananas when you actually bought clones of it made inside a science lab or something. I mean, a lot of commercials on TV always try to tell you what you should or shouldn't eat — but if you ask me, I think you're supposed to be the one to judge that yourself. I mean, just think about it — Mom's job is probably so boring because they're figuring out they can't judge people's supreme foods anymore," Ollie said.

"So then what supreme things are they doing?"

"Maybe they're figuring out how to be

supreme heroes in other ways now and help the world!" Ollie exclaimed.

"Well, one thing is for sure. You watch way too much TV — but I guess you make some good points. You are far beyond your years, Ollie."

"What's that supposed to mean?"

"I don't know. I heard Dad and Mom talking about you one day — that's all. Forget it. Anyway, back to what you said about food — today's the day you should be very careful with it," Joey warned.

"What do you mean?"

"I mean today is the day people are afraid of one thing — the food coma!" Joey yelled.

"What's that?" Ollie's voice was shaky.

"It means you go to sleep and can't wake up because you ate too much. Maybe you're already going through it since you said your stomach hurts from all the breakfast you had."

"But I ate the same amount as you!" Ollie protested with tears building in his eyes.

"Well, I'm older. Life works out better for me. So, anyway, do you want to look at the stuff from Mr. Café again?" Joey asked, ignoring the stream of tears now flowing down Ollie's face. Joey continued disregarding his brother's melodramatic facial expressions. "Oh, and I thought I smelled Dad baking. I don't know why he bakes gingerbread houses for Thanksgiving instead of leaving it all for

Christmas, but yeah. Oh, and I think we're going to Grandma's today because I heard Mom talking on the phone with Grandma last night." In turn, Ollie dismissed his brother's endless commentary by slamming the door on him again. "Cool orange shirt!" Joey yelled before walking away. Ollie looked down at his shirt that was clearly red, shrugged his shoulders, and went to tidy up his bed.

Now, walking further along the hallway, Joey tried to find something to fill the rest of his morning with. He settled on choosing to follow the sound of the voices he heard from afar. As he walked toward them, he found they were coming from the kitchen. There, he found his parents and dogs.

"You sure you don't want hot chocolate, Aria?" Justin asked.

"I will later. Not right now. 'Tis the season for my caffeine." Aria sipped her steaming cup of coffee.

"You know, chocolate has caffeine in it too," Justin replied. Aria rolled her eyes at her husband's desire to offer an alternative perspective during her mandatory coffee time. Justin immediately sensed the tense vibes coming from his wife and walked over to give her a quick hug. "But I know — 'Tis the season for me letting you do your thing." Aria nodded and continued flipping through her travel magazine as she drank. Across the way, Joey was playing with the dogs, but Aria and Justin were too preoccupied to notice him.

"Coffee," Aria said, "I like the feeling it gives me. I even like the color and taste of it whenever adding milk or cream to it. You know, I could be drinking this on top of the Eiffel Tower or even along the trails of Cinque Terre! I mean, there are just many ways you can have coffee — iced, or as a cake, or as a flavored ice cream — it's simply the epitome of versatility!" she laughed. "You can call me strange, but that just means you have to call all non-coffee lovers stranger." She smelled the aroma from her cup before taking another sip from it. Justin heard his wife's monologue, but wasn't exactly listening attentively enough to respond. He was busy looking for the best storage container to transfer the surplus of his gingerbread batter into. "Oh, I also wanted to tell you —" she began, but quickly became distracted by a surprising aroma filling the air. She scrunched her nose at the smell, then looked frantically toward the area where their double stacked ovens stood. "Justin, is something burning?" Joey smelled the burning smell too, but directed his attention at the nearby bay window. Sapphire and Jasper ran and aggressively barked at the window, but Justin ignored the barking and rushed from where he was at the kitchen island to the ovens where his masterpieces were. He grabbed his oven mitts so fast you would have thought he played professional baseball.

"No, there's nothing burning," Justin said, slowly closing up both oven doors.

"Wow, I thought I definitely smelled something," Aria replied, quietly wondering if she was losing her mind or simply needed a nap. "Sapphi, come sit with Mommy as she finishes her late morning coffee and dreams of being in Bora Bora." Sapphire jumped at Aria's command, leaving Jasper alone to peer out the window. Even though Joey sensed there was something outside, he decided ignoring it would be much more convenient for him today. With Sapphire's departure and Joey's lack of desire to investigate, Jasper found a spot where the sun was shining down on the floor the most and drifted off to sleep.

"Our weather is so emotional. It's usually raining but the minute the sun comes out, you'd think it was summer time. That's why the boys wear shorts so often — they think it'll eventually be summertime each day," Aria said.

"Yeah. They probably think if they wear shorts enough, it'll persuade the sun to stay shining and stop the curse of this sporadic rain," Justin laughed.

"Do you know how long those things are supposed to cook for?" Aria asked, squinting at the oven doors across the way.

"Forty minutes," Justin said, standing proudly.

"And how many minutes has it been?" Justin's face quickly dropped. He forgot to set a timer.

"I'm not much of a numbers person," he nonchalantly replied. They both quickly bursted into non stop laughter. Justin was absolutely the mathematician of the family. His passion for math somehow played a key role in his career as a therapist — most likely because math lovers are known to be the more emotionally stable people of our world. Even though Justin knew numbers and psychology were rather useful qualities to have, he couldn't help but wish they would directly help fight against the unexpected memory loss he also experienced. "Oh, you were saying you wanted to tell me something?"

"Oh, yes, thank you for actually remembering!"

"Aria, I don't forget all the time."

"That's right, dear. It's selective memory loss. Anywho, my mother wants us to go to her house today."

"Wow, talk about last minute," Justin said as he checked on his dishes baking inside the ovens.

"Well, she's been trying to get a hold of me about coming today for at least a few weeks now. Honestly, I've been debating on the topic."

"Of Thanksgiving?"

"Of being on the phone with her."

"It's your mother, Aria."

"I know, but c'mon, I'm up way too early and come home way too late to only be ankle deep in a conversation that stresses me out from her worrying that transpires into ridicule. This is every phone call with her."

"Then, text her."

"She won't text, Justin — and that's besides the point. This is who she is — especially whenever anyone is in person with her. Her judgements never stop. You know this."

"You make it seem like it doesn't bother you when you are in person with her, but I digress. Let's just set ourselves to leave here no later than in a couple of hours" Justin looked at the clock above the stove. "I'll make sure to get my masterpiece cooled off and decorated to take over." He began playing with the oven's brightness controls.

"Fine, that means I'll pack for everyone." Aria sighed as she got up from the table. Even though her mother wasn't the easiest woman to get along with, her husband was her sense of calm and always made the reunion with her tolerable. As Aria set Sapphire down on the floor, Jasper walked over and brushed up against her leg. She walked over to the kitchen island to grab two dog treats for them out of the jar. Sapphire gobbled hers up while Jasper carried his back to his crate. Jasper was the easiest dog to crate-train. Many dogs look at crates as jail, but Jasper saw it as his man cave. As Aria watched Jasper strut away, she turned back around to face Justin. "Mom's letting us spend the weekend there, so she said we can bring the dogs." Justin didn't respond. He was much too busy ensuring the pieces to his gingerbread creation weren't burning.

"Dude, we are going to Grandma's soon!" Joey said, sprinting from the kitchen into Ollie's bedroom. Ollie's room was completely rearranged with the most minimal amount of toys, books, and furniture pieces showing. "Woah, what happened to your room?" Ollie didn't respond. He was laying on top of his bed covers with his eyes closed. "Wake up!" Joey begged. Ollie continued laying very still, in an apparent deep sleep. "Well, I guess you really are in a food coma." Joey chuckled and shut the door behind him.

A Thankful Sleep At Grandma's ♉

Ollie never had a good perception of time. So, during the 2-hour drive to Grandma's house, he needed verification that they hadn't driven too long and missed Christmas Day.

"It's still Thanksgiving, Ollie," Joey rolled his eyes.

"Fine, then that explains why my tummy still hurts so much." Ollie continued groaning as he gazed through the car window.

"Well, like I said, be careful. It's National Food Coma Day," Joey snickered.

"Nuh-uh. It's Thanksgiving — you first said that!" Ollie snapped.

"Tomato-Potato," Joey shrugged as he pet Jasper who was calmly seated in between them.

"No, it's not about tomatoes and potatoes. It's about turkey and stuffing," Ollie said with his index finger held high.

"Look, I'm older so the things I say are automatically right every time!"

"Uh, the ancient Greeks called. They said your math doesn't add up. I'm the wiser one."

"Alright, boys, we are finally here," their father announced as they pulled up to a 3-story wooden house that was illuminated by its cherry red

colored door. The house had a fenced-in front yard
that fed into its backyard. As the car came to a stop,
Sapphire perked up from her seat on Aria's lap.
When the car doors opened, Sapphire leaped out
and ran around the big, grassy yard. Jasper
remained sitting still inside of the car, watching
everyone pile out before him. He waited until Justin
personally went over to him and encouraged him to
get out. As each of them approached the front door,
they were greeted by Amber, a ten pound Jack
Russell Terrier mix who had beige fur and the
highest IQ you'd ever experienced in a canine.
Although she was a dog, Amber responded to you
with human-like expressions. If you said something
immature and ignorant, she would look at you with
much dismay. Be that as it may, Amber loved
people, and simply, tolerated animals. As Aria,
Justin, Ollie, and Joey approached, she cheerfully
wagged her tail back and forth. Standing right
above her, leaning against a cane was Grandma
Jade. She was a tall, fit woman with long, dark
brown hair and wrinkles that were nonexistent.

"Happy Thanksgiving!" Grandma Jade
exclaimed, putting one hand in the air in lieu of a
physical hug. Having lived through many natural
disasters and global pandemics, Grandma Jade
found physical touching of many things unsanitary.
From refusing to eat grocery items packaged in

cardboard to wearing different shoes in front of the house than in the back, she did things the way she wanted to and scolded anyone for not following suit. She refrained from hugging, shaking hands, or giving high-fives to her own family members. She is witty as much as she is sharp. She has class but much more sass. "Now, hurry on inside. You're letting my heat out. I don't have the money to be heating up this whole town." Everyone hurried inside, piling into the dining room where they were greeted by a huge table of food. On one end, a roasted turkey glistened beautifully before them, and on the other, a fried turkey showed itself off by filling the air with a mouth-watering aroma. In the middle of the table was a delectable spread of cornbread stuffing, collard greens, baked yams, mashed sweet potatoes, roasted parmesan-garlic green beans, cranberry sauce, baked macaroni with gouda cheese, and an array of drinks. "Now, Olivia is supposed to be meeting us soon," she said while staring down at the buffet she prepared.

"Oh, you talked to her?" Aria asked as she sat in a chair off to the side.

"Why are you sitting there? Sit at the table! Sit in that chair right there!" Aria jumped up at her mother's command.

"Sorry, I didn't know where you wanted me to sit — and I didn't want to sit in your seat," Aria said, looking down at her heels. Justin put his hand on her shoulder and sat in the seat beside her. The boys quickly chose their seats, knowing their grandmother well enough to wait before serving themselves. Grandma Jade left the dining room and motioned for all the dogs to sit in a room located diagonally from them. Depending on where you were sitting at the dining room table, you could see the furniture that livened up the doorless dog room across the way. Grandma Jade wandered around the room, trying to find a portable fence that would be sturdy enough to discourage the dogs from getting out.

"I'm going to put those suitcases away before she thinks we planned to leave them in a noncompliant area," Justin said with a smirk on his face, looking at their luggage collected off to the side. As he left, Aria reached for a glass sitting in the middle of the table.

"Do you want juice?" Aria asked the boys, pointing to the group of juice boxes sitting before them.

"No, I want water," Ollie moaned.

"Honey, what's the matter?" Aria asked.

"His tummy hurts. He already had his food coma for the day, so he's a lost cause," Joey replied, reaching for a juice box.

"It's been hurting since this morning," Ollie whimpered.

"What could it have been? Did I undercook the french toast? It can't be the yogurt, could it?" she gasped. As Aria pondered, Ollie continued moaning. "Honey let's get you laid down." Aria walked him to the room he'd be bunking in with his brother, and snuggled him into the bed closest to the door. "Lay here and ring that bell if you need me." She pointed to a bell resting on a wooden nightstand before exiting the room. Ollie glanced at it before closing his eyes and falling asleep.

"Where's Oliver?" Grandma Jade asked with intense worry as Aria found her seat back at the dining room table.

"He's not feeling well and went to bed," Aria replied meekly.

"I wish I could go back to bed. What's wrong with him?" she snarled.

"I'm not sure, but he said his stomach hurts."

"The child probably doesn't get enough nutrition." Grandma Jade sat back in her chair, closely watched Aria take a sip from her glass and completely miss her mouth. Aria gasped, startled by both the spill she had made and the doorbell suddenly ringing.

"That's probably your sister," Grandma Jade said, getting up from the table. "But I can't answer it until I get this mess you made cleaned up."

"No, you don't need to, Mother. I will absolutely do it."

"You don't know how! You don't know how to do anything!"

"Listen, I will get the door and you can rest," Justin said, looking at Grandma Jade. Aria looked at her husband before getting up to fetch the rather unusual tools her mother expected messes to be cleaned up with. These tools included a toothbrush, a cotton ball, and her mother's homemade cleaning solution. This miracle solution that was stored in an old peanut butter jar was believed to be mostly made of soap and water.

"I like that man," Grandma Jade said, as she poured herself a glass of juice and supervised her daughter's cleaning. "I might just go back to bed after I finish this glass because you all are already tiring me out."

"I know, Mother," Aria said while scrubbing with the world's tiniest, inefficient toothbrush.

"The party's here!" Aunt Olivia announced, entering the room with her hands held high. Aria was still very upset with her sister, so she did not look up from her cleaning to greet her.

"Hi, Aunt Olivia!" Joey perked up happily from his chair. Aunt Olivia scurried over to hug him.

"Where is your brother?" she asked.

"He's in bed," Joey said.

"Well, he might have the right idea by how this dinner might turn out," she whispered. She blew air kisses at the barking dogs who had no idea who she was.

"Did you forget what time you were expected here? You were supposed to get here twelve hours ago to help me cook. How forgetful, or rather, how lazy can you be?" Grandma Jade stared at her with fire in her eyes. Olivia opened her mouth to defend herself, but couldn't find the words. "Olivia, I had to get out of bed sooner than I needed to because you chose to do what you wanted to and let me be here all stressed."

"Alright, well, it seems you've made up your mind about what happened and wish to be in a snappy mood, but I will maintain my peace, joy, and desire to give everyone here a Thanksgiving hug." Olivia hugged and complimented each person, one by one. "So, is everyone ready to eat?"

"We are saying *grace*," Grandma Jade snapped. Everyone grabbed their neighbor's hand, closed their eyes, and bowed their heads. "Thank you, Lord, for the food we are about to receive.

May you cleanse it with any and all its impurities, bless my being the only hands that truly prepared it, and thank you for the means of providing it. Also, may no one attempt to try me so I don't go off on anyone in Jesus' name, Amen."

"Amen," everyone said in unison.

After the feast, Joey was on clean up duty. Part of this duty was to make and deliver a plate of food to Ollie in bed. Joey thought it would be funny to put all but turkey on the plate, so he did just that. Although, his mother caught him and made him add more turkey than he could ever imagine to the plate.

Carrying the hot dish in one hand, and a juice box in the other, Joey entered the bedroom where Ollie was still fast asleep. He studied his little brother, wanting to make sure he was still breathing comfortably before setting the plate of food on a dresser. The steam from the plate filled the room with such an appetizing smell, you might've thought the furniture would come to life to take a bite. Joey anticipated the aroma would wake his brother, causing him to receive the high kudos he believed he deserved for being so generous with the turkey portion. Although, to his dismay, Ollie continued resting in deep slumber. Suddenly, from his peripheral vision, Joey saw the shadows of two men outside the window. He looked again and saw nothing. He shrugged it off, convinced he must be sugar deprived and in need of one of the many desserts back in the kitchen. Ignoring the color red beaming around both the window and Ollie, Joey took a piece of turkey from his brother's plate. On his way out, he disregarded the color orange that was also following him as he munched away.

A Dream To Pay Attention To ♋

Inside the apartment building, there were several units that had the same brown wooden door. Without hesitation, Ollie opened the one that had the most wood chippings on it. The chippings gave the door character. More than anything, its wear and tear represented the door's durability. On the other side of the door was a woman stirring a large tin of steaming water in the middle of the kitchen floor.

"It's Saturday night, sugar," the woman said. "Don't look so confused. What do we do every Saturday night?" The woman had long, brown hair, olive skin, and high cheekbones. She was wearing a burgundy, long sleeved blouse, along with an ankle-length dark green skirt.

"You are a gentleman and a scholar," a man said, entering through the front door behind Ollie. It was the man from earlier who told Ollie to go up the stairs. The man tossed the newspaper he had in his hand off to the side and placed his hat on a wall hook before turning to Ollie. "I just spoke with Mr. Jackson today. He said you are doing mighty fine down at the warehouse." Ollie smiled, hoping the smile was believable enough to hide the mountain of fear he had. "Now, I seem to have dropped my monocle," the man said, scanning the floor. "Did you see it on me earlier?"

"No," Ollie said meekly, clearing his throat.

"You lose that thing like you lose your mind," the woman said to the man. "Now, come on and get in this bath." She motioned for Ollie to get inside the large tin of water after feeling the water with the back of her hand. "The water is at a good temperature now." Despite being confused by being asked to bathe like a dog in the middle of the kitchen, Ollie did as he was told. While he approached the large silver pail, the man and woman walked out of sight to the opposite end of the home. He could hear them speaking but couldn't make out the words they were saying. Ollie unbuttoned each large brown button of the long wool coat he had been wearing. He had a simple red t-shirt and black pants underneath. He left them on and decided to only remove the shoes and socks from his feet. He was much too afraid and too cold to completely submerge himself into the water and relax. He stood soaking his feet inside the tin for one full minute before bending down to scoop water into his hands to warm his freezing face. He then looked around him. The home was small and very well kept. There was a solid wood hand carved table with four matching chairs in the kitchen, and a smaller table with two stools underneath it in the living room area. Next to it was a tall case clock ticking back and forth. As Ollie studied the clock, he noticed its reflection in the glass top of a nearby dresser. He continued looking around, puzzled by there not being a television, ceiling fan, or light switch anywhere in sight. There were, however, pictures of the man, the woman, and himself on the walls and shelves. As he studied the photographs closest to him, he became both frightened and intrigued by the strangers posing next to him. After many minutes of studying, Ollie stepped out of the water and dried his feet and face with the towel that was nicely folded on the ground. He didn't know where he was or why he was there. Be that as it may, the dropped temperature redirected his attention to putting his socks back on, and going to peer outside the window. As he did, snow began to fall, but this peaceful observation was short lived due to the ruckus coming from the people living in the above unit. They were talking loudly while moving various furniture pieces. The apartment unit shook anytime someone in the building opened and closed the main entry door several floors below. As he directed his attention back outside the window, he studied the area below where he had originally met the man. He saw many people now occupying that area, scurrying to various destinations before nightfall. Street vendors were selling the last of their produce before closing. As he looked at another building across the way, he noticed how much lower off the ground it stood. It was as if it were sinking. Its roof looked as though it would rip off with the slightest gust of wind. As confused as he was about this entire place, Ollie felt a sense of safety and security in the apartment unit. He watched the sun set, witnessing the room becoming dark. The front door creaked open by what Ollie believed to be the wind. He looked back at the building across the way to see if its roof was still attached, but got distracted by the sound of footsteps. When the footsteps stopped, he calmed his nerves by watching the snow continue to fall. A big snowflake suddenly hit his window. Ollie jumped back, tripped over a floor rug, and fell to the ground.

"You alright, champ? You seem awfully quiet and startled by things today," the man said, having appeared out of nowhere.

"George, let him have his peace," the woman said, closing the ajar front door. Ollie felt great pain from his fall and felt something continuing to hurt him. From his back pocket, he pulled out a shiny, gold linked chain object.

"My monocle!" the man exclaimed. "How did you find it?"

"Just saw it here when I fell," Ollie replied meekly. The man gently took it from him and placed it over his eye. "You are truly a gentleman and a scholar. This here is an heirloom from your grandfather, Gary. That is why we named you after him — Garysson. You and this thing are the only things I care about in this world." From across the room, the woman shot him a spiteful look. "Oh, and of course you, dear," he quickly added.

"Yes, well you can wash up while there's still some heat left in that tub, and I will get our son here into bed." The woman helped Ollie up and motioned for him to walk with her through the narrow hallway. She took him to a room with a small bed that had a nightstand next to it. On top of the nightstand was a lit candle. There wasn't much room for anything else in the dark wooden paneled room. "Now, it's almost Christmas and we have many more neckties to make in the morning. Say your prayers and blow your fire out right after." As the woman closed the door, Ollie immediately blew the candle out and closed his eyes. He began to pray in pitch darkness. He had a lot of questions for God — more questions than there was candle wax left to burn.

A Big Talk With Mr. Café ∞

"Ollie! Don't make me call you Oliver!" Joey yelled as he hovered over his sleeping little brother. It was daylight now and Ollie saw that he was back in the last place he truly knew he was supposed to be — his grandmother's house. "You slept all night and wouldn't wake up. Why are you in such deep sleeps all the time now?" Joey asked. Amber jumped up on the bed to greet Ollie whose stomach was feeling much better now. In fact, his stomach was rumbling. He could hear the clinking of glasses and sizzling of meat in the kitchen across the way. Ollie followed the smell where he was met with a hefty serving of thick turkey slices and scrambled eggs. This was the traditional breakfast his family had every year before they went Black Friday shopping. Ollie wanted time alone to ponder about his recent dreams, so he carried his plate to a table out of ear shot, but not out of sight, from the main kitchen area.

"So, anyway, that's why I won't be Black Friday shopping this year," Aunt Olivia said, finishing her turkey and taking a sip of her coffee.

"Do you want any milk or juice to drink?" Grandma Jade looked at Justin.

"I'll take juice, thank you. Milk just makes me queasy and stuff" Justin replied.

"Poor Aria," Olivia teased.

"No — poor Aria for not getting any sleep last night because of Justin's constant need to converse," Aria replied.

"What?" Justin questioned before gulping down his juice.

"You were up talking to me as if we were mid convo already. I told you to go back to sleep, but you proceeded to get up and walk around the room. I couldn't make out what you were physically doing because we were in pitch darkness. So, I left you to it."

"Why didn't you turn on the light?" Grandma Jade asked sharply.

"You don't allow bedroom lights on at night," Aria said meekly.

"Yeah, that is very true. Makes no sense burning up my electricity bill when God gave you the moon and your five senses to go on and do what you need to when facing darkness," Grandma Jade said while continuing to clean the same dishes for the third time.

"Mom, you have the outdoor lights on all the time," Olivia chuckled.

"That's my business. My domain. My rules," she replied sharply.

"Yeah, I get it. Bills never seem to go down," Aria sighed.

"Yeah, and you all being here makes sure of that," Grandma Jade scoffed.

"Mom, we are your family who you invited here and now you are chastising us all for being here! Bedroom lights are supposed to be used — especially at night," Olivia replied.

"Tell that to the people living in the old days. They had to figure out the hour of the day and plan their day based on the sun and moon hovering right there above their God-given heads," Grandma Jade said as she dried off her hands.

"Yeah, life happens while you're living it," Aria said as she wiped down the table.

"Well, I'm thrilled Alessandro Volta, Humphry Davy, Warren de la Rue, William Staite, Joseph Swan, and *then* Thomas Edison took a walk on the wild side to give us our light bulb today." Olivia drank the last of her coffee then stared at the lamp above her head. Grandma Jade looked blankly at Olivia then at the lamp.

"Wow, I didn't know it took that many people to create the light bulb," Justin said.

"Oh, that's just the few we know. A lot of things are only credited to one person when that is far from the truth. It takes a village!" Aria replied.

"Amen," Grandma Jade replied as she quickly walked over to the nearby Carlton House desk and opened a drawer to retrieve a hairbrush. Everyone pretended they didn't notice her instant calling to tame her long, wavy mane. Fortunately, if there was one thing Olivia took pride in, it was diverting from any awkward moment in order to keep everyone entertained.

"Anyway, Justin, how strange of you to be sleep-talking, walking, and all that, right?"

"I just think your sister is making a mistake and is just too filled up on turkey from yesterday. I was fast asleep the whole night," he laughed.

"You are truly delusional," Aria rolled her eyes and smiled.

"You all are just under a lot of stress at those jobs. You need better rest," Grandma Jade said, placing her hairbrush in the pocket of her apron before returning to the sink.

"I can help you with the dishes, Mom," Olivia said, approaching the kitchen sink.

"No, you don't know how to do it!" she snapped. She then cleared her throat, untied her apron, and looked at each of them, one-by-one. "Let me explain the rules of my house to each of you. Then, afterward, I will follow in my youngest grandson's footsteps from yesterday and spend the rest of the day in bed, OK? First and foremost, water cannot go down any of my drains. Instead, you are to collect water in its respective nearby bucket. Nothing is or ever has been wrong with my drains, but I believe that is because I am taking care of them properly by not using them. The use of drains are for the weak and most ill-mannered kind of people. To use them is to misuse them. What if they get rusty or clogged? I can't afford to even think about what that bill will be! Secondly, whenever you leave my house and return to it, you are to immediately go into the shower or, at the very least, change your clothes. I don't want you bringing outside germs into my domain and exposing me to unnecessary bacteria. I noticed neither of you cared to do that before we ate our holiday meal yesterday. The improper home practices you exercise are a poor reflection on me."

"Mother, how are we supposed to know those are your rules if you have never told them to us?" Aria asked meekly.

"I'm speaking," Grandma Jade calmly replied as she got her hairbrush out to use as a baton in order to conduct the finale of her speech. "Lastly, nothing goes on the top shelf of anything. I feel that using the top shelves of anything welcomes disaster. Things can collapse and hurt you from up there."

"When has that ever happened to you?" Aria asked with more power in her voice.

"Never — but it happened to my friend once. So, if it happened to her, it can happen to me or to you. These rules are the ingredients to living smarter, not harder. It's called living in wisdom."

"No, it's called living in fear," Olivia replied.

"Well, I'll be mature enough to admit I worry sometimes. I've just been through a lot — but if I hug you and serve you cookies every waking moment, you might forget to have thick skin! Plus, hugs, themselves, are invitations for germs."

"Well, I for one, love cookies so I wouldn't mind," Justin said smiling to break the tension, but everyone resorted to awkwardly looking at inanimate objects around them.

"I fear it's just too late to improve from my ways," Grandma Jade sighed after a few moments sitting in silence.

"No, no. Like I tell plaintiffs and defendants alike, it's never too late to better yourself. You just need the will to stay improved," Aria said.

"Whatever. I'm going to bed," Grandma Jade said as she abruptly left the kitchen.

"So, does that mean I need to go change? I mean, I must have germs on me after I went to go grab something out of my car this morning," Olivia chuckled, hoping to ease the tension in the room.

"Well, from *your* car, I wouldn't put it past you," Aria laughed. Justin then went to search for his cell phone that was ringing in a different part of the house, leaving Olivia and Aria alone for what they felt to be a very long time.

"You know, living in fear gives you age lines and sleeping too much gives you unnecessary pillow wrinkles. You should really get Oliver checked out," Olivia said, turning their silence into genuine laughter with one another. In the middle of them wiping their tears of joy, Justin called Aria's name. As she got up from her chair, Ollie walked over, passing his Aunt Olivia. She smiled, looked him deep in his eyes, and pinched his cheeks. He didn't understand why she had the sudden urge to do that, but shrugged it off and journeyed back to the bedroom.

In the bedroom, Joey was playing tug-of-war with Jasper. Ollie walked to the foot of the bed, fell backward, and let out a deep sigh. He was still thinking a lot about his dreams and the fact he couldn't make sense of any of it. Jasper greeted Ollie by putting his wet nose to his foot and pawing the back of his hand.

"Hey! What's that?" Joey said, pointing to a paper bag behind the bedroom door. Ollie maneuvered Jasper off of him to look at what his brother was pointing at.

"Oh, it's just my bag from Mr. Café," Ollie shrugged. Joey went underneath his bed covers to reveal his paper bag.

"I brought mine too," he smiled. "Wanna look through them again?"

"OK," Ollie sighed. As he walked over to retrieve his bag, Ollie had flashbacks of both the moment they met Mr. Café, the moment in his dream where he met the man with the monocle.

"Ollie, are you OK?" Joey asked, waving his hands in front of his brother's face.

"What? Oh, yeah. Um..."

"It's fine. Everyone needs to zone out once in a while. Anyway, I'm going to tell you something, but you can't say I'm weird or else you owe me $1."

"But I don't have a dollar."

"Then, make sure you don't make fun of me," Joey replied while emptying his bag.

"OK, what is it?"

"See these glasses? I put them on the other night and saw stuff. Like, if I decide to pay attention to it, I can always see colors and numbers around me. Honestly, I see colors a lot when I hear or think about music! It's weird though because when I was talking to Jasper, I had these glasses on and there was no music playing. I don't know! It's weird!"

"You sure your elbow wasn't the only thing you injured after falling that day?" Ollie laughed.

"I told you to not make fun!"

"You're the one who kept saying it was weird!"

"Whatever, little old boy!" Joey crossed his arms and turned away from his brother.

"OK, but seriously — maybe you were dreaming because I feel like sometimes when I dream, I'm in a different life or something." Ollie studied the socks from Mr. Café he had balled up in his hand.

"What's that got to do with anything I just said about me?"

"I don't know, but maybe everything Mr. Café gave us is helping us see things better. For me, all my weird dreams happened after we met Mr. Café, and now you're telling me those glasses have you talking to our dog! So, think about it!"

"Maybe we should just go back to Mr. Café and ask him all about this!" Just then, Aria and Justin walked through the door. The boys looked up at their parents' stressed faces.

"Boys, we're going to leave now instead of tomorrow. We have some things to care for at home." Aria sipped the last of her coffee. "Your father will help you pack." She stared sternly at Justin before walking away.

Sapphire and Jasper were already fast asleep as they pulled out of Grandma Jade's driveway.

"I can't believe the dogs are knocked out like this! You'd think they just got done working a nine-to-five job or something," Aria laughed.

"Yeah. They've been sleeping a lot more. You'd think they were working for Corporate America," Justin laughed.

"Maybe your treat you left would have kept them up more. I think it's fascinating you've mastered making an edible gingerbread house for dogs."

"Yeah, but I'm still kicking myself for forgetting to bring it," Justin replied.

"Well, don't beat yourself up. It's the first year you've forgotten to bring your annual holiday creation — but we definitely can't afford for you to forget anything more. We don't want you relapsing back to things."

"I know, but I still think I should stop suppressing all of this, Aria," Justin replied.

"There are pros and cons either way, dear." Aria looked out the window and watched a plane travel in the cloudy sky above.

"Yeah, I suppose stranger things have happened," Justin sighed. "But, ya know, maybe my subconscious is truly telling me to go for it — and that must have been why I was up all night!"

"Oh, so now you admit you were awake?" Aria chuckled, then looked through the rearview mirror at Ollie. "Oh, Oliver, your brother made you your Thanksgiving plate. I put it in the cooler, alongside some chocolate chip cookies Grandma Jade made last minute."

"Yeah, little brother, so you owe me your next turkey sandwich for all the thankless work I did putting your plate together," Joey said. "And since I charge interest, I will be taking all of your cookies as partial payment."

"I don't owe you anything!" Ollie cried.

"What do you know about interest, Joseph?" Justin laughed. "I guess Joseph is wise beyond his years too," Justin whispered to Aria.

"They both are — just in different ways," she smiled back, still watching the clouds very closely.

"So, should we ask Mom and Dad if we can go?" Ollie whispered to Joey.

"No, you do it!"

"No, you!"

"I'm older!"

" I'm wiser!" Ollie replied.

"OK, great! So, you can go take your wise self over there and ask them if we can go," Joey replied.

"Fine, but I'm only doing it because I don't want to hear your mouth anymore!" Ollie exclaimed. Ollie gave a convincing speech to his parents who agreed they could have a quick visit to the café. Although, it came at the price of their mother spending the rest of the ride lecturing them on the importance of time management.

Inside the café, Ollie and Joey found Mr. Café cleaning. The place was less lively than before. In fact, there was not a customer in sight. Mr. Café was tidying things up underneath counters and behind shelves.

"Mr. Café!" Ollie exclaimed. Startled by the noise, Mr. Café bumped his head while cleaning cake crumbs off the ground. He rubbed his head with his left hand — the only currently clean hand he had — before standing up and smiling.

"Well, hi!" he said. "I needed a break here anyway." He washed his hands, went to a small, hidden freezer and got an ice pack out. He wrapped the ice pack in paper towels before putting it to his head. "Come. Let's sit over here." He motioned for them to sit at a table against one of the walls.

"Our parents are outside and they said we can't stay long, but we have questions." Joey revealed his notebook and sunglasses. Ollie pointed to the watch and socks he was wearing.

"I know you do." Mr. Café closed his eyes, trying to fight an inevitable brain freeze.

"You do?" Joey was shocked.

"The minute you sat down at that table over there the other day, I knew you two were close to tapping in." The boys didn't respond. They didn't understand what he meant. "I know this is confusing, but just understand that everyone has a sixth sense," he said as he put the ice pack down. Ollie sat as frozen as the ice pack on the table. "People think and only teach you how to use and control five of your senses, but we indeed have six. Sometimes, we have even more — but I'd still rule them all under having a sixth sense. Anyway, it's your job to discover it. On the surface, the senses wear differently on each of us, but there's a lot more similarities we have to one another than we're willing to admit. It's your job to unleash your sixth sense and start your part in saving humanity from itself. You know, the jealous, the disapproving, and the unforgiving washing machine cycle we're stuck in is just a preposterous waste of time." The boys didn't understand what he meant, but they kept listening. "Alright, so, there are people who have the ability to see color. They can correlate the things around them with numbers — or even smell things the world would otherwise deem unsmellable. These people are called Synesthetes." He walked behind the counter to put his ice pack back inside the freezer and threw away the now very damp paper towels. "Now, this is all part of discovering how everyone and everything has a greater worth. Synesthetes understand everything in life being connected to one another. So, hating your neighbor, as I said before, is a waste of time when we're all here to be one team, you see? You can do so much more by loving one another and educating yourself on different cultures. That's the only way the pandemic we're currently in will deplete."

"What pandemic are we currently in?" Joey asked.

"A pandemic of resentment amongst mankind," he replied. Even though he didn't understand, Joey nodded and aimlessly turned his attention to the wall art that had recently been rearranged. "I can see you're not following me so let me take a step back. Alright, why do you think we accept having allergies in response to the nature around us? Why aren't we focusing on figuring out how to minimize natural disasters? I mean, we just rule each disaster as being inevitable. While it may be true for some of them, it isn't true for every single one. I say all this to explain how we neglect the very foundation and fundamental reason for us being alive on this planet." The boys looked at him blankly as he prepared to continue his lecture. "This planet is filled with water. You know it started out that way. Then, the land we're resting our feet on right now came about. Anyway, boys, just understand that Synesthetes are the epitome of what it means to be peaceful, forward-thinking humans who care for all things in all ways." Ollie and Joey continued wearing blank looks on their faces. "Now, interestingly, people close to tapping into their synesthesia ability are those who happen to be left-handed." He laughed and held up his left hand. As he did, he exposed a plus sign tattoo on his upper arm. "I know it sounds strange, but many people see being left-handed as something unique, abnormal, rare — however you want to spin it — but you should understand that those with a dominant left hand have subconsciously taken the first step into defying the common societal belief that the right hand is the *right* hand. I mean, we place our right hands over our hearts, most towns drive on the right side of the road, we greet people with our right hand — isn't that right?" He laughed as he shoveled items onto a tray and walked from behind the counter with a vanilla-caramel sundae for Joey and a bowl of banana pudding for Ollie. After the boys tasted their desserts, Mr. Café sat down at their table. "Now, with proper self-revelations from training, Synesthetes will teach others how being ambidextrous is the ultimate goal in life." He smiled down at his hands. "Because everything is truly connected, right?" He laughed as he stood up and walked behind the counter where a case of pastries sat on display.

"What are some other senses and abilities, Mr.Café?" Ollie fed himself a large spoonful of pudding.

"Well, there are the Animal Whisperers, the Time Jumpers, and —".

"But how many things can one person be?" Joey interrupted as he smacked caramel sauce off his lips.

"Well, that's up to the person," Mr. Café replied. "How much effort are they willing to put in, you know? Some people make great progress with finding their abilities right after being born, but over time, suppress it all by allowing outside teachings to take over. Although, most of us — even the so-called smart ones — only use ten percent of the brain. I find that the younger you start living, the easier it is to live. So, my recommendation for you two is to start being conscientious and attentive to things. There's power behind the questions you have. As you find them though, get in the habit of asking what you can do for life instead of thinking life always has to do something for you."

"What do you mean?" Joey asked.

"Your decisions are one-hundred percent your responsibility," Mr. Café replied.

"I think I get it," Ollie said, looking aimlessly at the ceiling.

"Good. You should be in good shape then because everyone always says people are born for a reason, but very few people go and find that reason. They just repeat one inspirational quote after the other before going back to their stressful lives. Sure, they'll make sure to pencil in exercising or book a vacation for some relaxation, but what they don't realize is that they are only treating the stresses they have instead of curing them. You probably know some grown ups that do that. So, as you go on, remember that doing the same thing over and over and expecting different results is the definition of insanity. That's why you need to focus on bettering yourself rather than gossiping about how someone else should've bettered themselves."

"I'll definitely remember that and keep reminding everyone at school about that too!" Joey exclaimed.

"Joey, did you hear what I just said? Focus on bettering yourself. You need to live a life that teaches people how to fish instead of giving them a whole bunch of fish."

"Don't worry, Mr. Café, Joey doesn't even have one fish," Ollie said.

"What I mean is repeating those uplifting messages to one another without personally living that life yourself doesn't prove anything more than your mastery of the English language." Mr. Café threw the black, red, orange, and blue striped rag he had in his hand over his shoulder. "People allow the media to control how they should feel, how they should grow up, and what age they need to do it by. Those biased directives take you off your path. Think about it. Your calling could have come to you at two years old, while mine might have come at six months old — but the media tells you not to worry about such and such until you get to a certain age. That's why each generation is taking longer and longer to reach their actual calling. Not to mention, we have turned the differences and talents of others into reasons to ridicule and condemn — and if that mockery frustrates you to the point you stop following your destiny, well, you robbed yourself of your own path." At this point, the boys had stopped eating and were sitting on the edge of their seats. "I know you guys are young, but I see you as mature enough to understand this, so let me tell you this — the people of this world would live a lot longer, and be a lot more fulfilled if they learned how to actually live it. There'd be a lot less crimes, a lot less judgmental people, and a lot more forgiveness and appreciation."

"What are you supposed to do when you figure out what your sixth sense is?" Ollie asked as he played with his spoon.

"Well, that's between you and God — part of your reason for being," Mr. Café replied.

"How do you even know which sixth sense you have?" Joey asked.

"Well, once you pay attention to your abilities. There are absolutely signs — symptoms — as I like to call them. So, paying attention to those will help."

"What are the symptoms?" Joey asked.

"Well, if you're a Synesthete, you of course, see color but you may see those colors based on your perception of the energy around it instead of what the energy and its color truly is. So, you'll have to teach yourself to see truth, not fantasy. Oh, and sometimes a Synesthete has a great fear of heights. Now, for the Animal Whisperers, well, they sometimes have a symptom of being afraid of the ocean — but as I'm saying all this, understand that symptoms vary by person." Ollie and Joey re-positioned their seating as they listened. "It's fascinating though — Animal Whisperers can talk to any animal they set their minds to. Although, if they have that notorious symptom of being afraid of the ocean, well, those sea creatures don't get much attention, do they? Anyway, then you have those

Time Jumpers — well, their symptoms tend to revolve around sleep-walking, sleep-talking, and sleep-paralysis. Interestingly enough, they tend to be lactose intolerant too."

"Boys!" their mother snapped from the doorway.

"Oh, man! We have a lot more questions, Mr. Café! How did you know to give *me* the bag with the sunglasses in it?" Joey asked as he quickly collected his things from the table.

"Yeah, and what's the point of me getting socks?" Ollie asked as he rose from his chair and showed off his footwear.

"Alright, boys, well, I hope those dog treats helped, and I hope you end up enjoying that notebook and that watch too," Mr. Café calmly replied as he headed toward the table they were departing from.

"But how did you know what to give us?" Joey asked with great enthusiasm, walking backward toward the door.

"Well, when you get to be my age, having started as young as I did, you just have a hunch. Oh, and none of this is magic." The boys watched Mr. Café quickly clear the table and return behind the counter as they continued their slow walk to the door.

"Were the blankets you gave us part of this non-magical stuff too?" Ollie yelled after him. After soon realizing they would not be getting an answer, the boys looked at one another with confusion. As Joey turned his head to face his mother, he saw the color red beaming all around her.

A Sec To Organize The Mess ♂

"So, my head hurts and I still don't get it," Ollie stated.

"What's there not to get?" Joey asked.

The boys were in Joey's room. No matter how messy it got, Joey always thought of his room as an organized mess. The boys managed to push some of the mess off to the side, so they could sit on the rug and analyze the gifts from Mr. Café.

"Why did you toss the empty plastic dog treat bag over there?" Ollie asked.

"Oh, I made an executive decision to throw it out."

"Why is your definition of throwing something out not in a trash can?"

"Alright, let's move on. So, according to Mr. Café, I'm an Animal Whisperer, right?"

"Right, but are you also afraid of heights?" Ollie asked.

"I don't know. I missed my sky diving appointment," Joey teased.

"Well, I also found out things about me from our talk with him."

"Oh yeah? What?"

"That I think I'm a Time Jumper because I have trouble sleeping. Oh, and I absolutely lack toast and tall mints," Ollie replied.

"No, no. It's lactose intolerant — like the label on your dessert that day said."

"Oh, well we still don't know what that even means."

"I know what it means!

"Oh, yeah?"

"Yeah! I went to go find the answer while you were busy sleeping one day. Yep, Dad told me all about it! He said lactose intolerant means you're allergic to the sugar that's inside of milk. Personally, I think that's a very sad way to live, but then again, having an entire dairy allergy is even sadder. Ehh, well, I don't know. Both of them suck."

"Thanks for that," Ollie said, rolling his eyes.

"Hey, it's not *my* fault you're going through what you're going through — but I will always look out for you. It's both my responsibility and my choice to do so as your big brother."

"Thanks. You are a gentleman and a scholar," Ollie replied with a big smile.

"Huh?"

"Nothing — err, anyway, what should we do now?"

"Well, even though I guess I don't really get a lot of this either, we should just move forward and focus on understanding one of our sixth senses better. Let's start with yours."

"Wow. Thanks!"

"Yep, so you gotta go to sleep!" Joey threw his royal blue comforter at Ollie's face.

"Stop! I can't just go to sleep like that!" Ollie pretended he was going to get back at Joey and throw the comforter at his face, but tossed it almost perfectly back onto the bed.

"OK, Ollie, let's continue. I wonder if our sixth senses are meant to work together. It's important we figure this out now." Joey stared at the colors he saw on his rug.

"What do you mean by now?" Ollie asked.

"I mean, we need to start understanding what all this means *now*, while we're still young."

"Uh-uh, don't act like you're all that young. I'm the young one — young and wise," Ollie replied.

"Yeah, yeah, whatever. OK, maybe I need to start writing down the conversations I have with Jasper, and the things I feel whenever I see colors and stuff," Joey picked up and studied his notebook.

"Oh, that's a good idea!" Ollie exclaimed.

"Yeah, just me and my two super senses."

"Joey, it's sixth sense."

"That's not what Mr. Café said!"

"Yes, it is."

"Well, it's not what I remember him saying."

"Well, Mom always says both you and Dad have selective memory."

"Well, that's my business."

"OK, well, even though I think Mr. Café said all abilities fall under having a sixth sense, I'll play your game and talk things out as though you have *two* kinds of sixth senses," Ollie sighed.

"Perfect," Joey replied.

"I just can't believe you have two abilities for your sixth senses. I mean, I don't even know my one!" Ollie cried.

"Don't be jealous."

"I'm not."

"Jealousy is just love and hate at the same time."

"I'm not jealous. I'm blessed," Ollie replied.

"Well, I'm truly blessed in all of my mess." Joey looked around his unorganized room with pride.

"Well, just don't lose any of your sixth senses in here like you probably lose the back of your hand in all this mess!"

"Well, God gave me another hand for backup," Joey said with a shrug.

"Don't live life on the edge like that."

"Hey, my domain, my rules!" Joey replied.

"What's a domain?" Ollie asked.

"I don't know. Grandma Jade says it a lot. Anyway, as I was saying, before I was rudely interrupted, I can write down all of the stuff we experience here in this notebook." Joey studied the label on the notebook closely. "What do you think 'Left-handed+' means — like what do you think they are saying left-handed people add to?"

"My stress level," Ollie said, lightly massaging his head.

"No, seriously, I think it has to do with that big, Amber-sounding word."

"Aww, Amber!" Ollie exclaimed as he got up to throw away the empty dog treat bag his brother carelessly had off to the side.

"Yeah, well, maybe that big word is actually her full name and 'Amber' is just a nickname."

"Her name has nothing to do with a person named Nick!" Ollie snapped.

"I digest. Anyway, I forgot what that Amber-sounding word was." Joey was ignoring the cleaning his brother was now doing around him. "OK, well, I at least remember what Mr. Café said about that Amber word." Joey picked up a pen and began writing in his notebook using his right hand. "I think this is what we both need to do."

"Yeah! You can do that, but you also need to be cleaning this place up," Ollie replied.

"No, no. I need to write in this book using my right hand and you need to wear that watch on your left."

"Why?" Ollie sat back down on the rug with his brother.

"Well, because those are the opposite hands we mostly use, so we need to work on using them, and practice being 'Amber' about the whole thing."

"No problem. We hardly get to see her. I can honor Amber that way."

"Yeah, she's awesome! She and I had fun playing while you were busy sleeping at Grandma's all of Thanksgiving," Joey replied.

"So, did you have an actual talk with her like you did with Jasper?"

"No. I decided to take a recess from all of that."

"Wait — what do you mean by recess? You weren't at school." Ollie squinted at his brother.

"I don't know. I hear Mom say that a lot. I think she has recesses a lot at work."

"Well, that's good for her. It's very boring inside her supreme world judge job. She needs recess," Ollie replied.

"Yeah, and the more I thought about taking a recess from talking to the dogs, the more I thought about going into retirement altogether," Joey sighed.

"Retirement?" Ollie questioned.

"Yeah, when you get to be my age, then you'll understand," Joey replied.

"Well, speaking of re-tired, I'm getting tired."

"No, no. You had the opportunity to sleep. Now, we need to work."

"Why can't we go have recess?"

"I don't know what your point is. It's not like you sleep at recess," Joey replied.

"Whatever." Ollie began rubbing his eyes and yawning.

"OK, so, we need to break everything down and connect the dots." As Joey reached for a pen, Ollie threw the bed comforter at him. Unbothered by his brother's tantrum, Joey began writing in his notebook. "So, like I said, I can keep track of things in this notebook. I promise to write using my right hand — or at least hold my notebook in my right hand," he chuckled.

"It would honestly behoove you to at least do that much," Ollie scoffed.

"What does 'behoove' mean?" Joey asked.

"I don't know. That word just came out of me all of a sudden."

"You are one weird little dude," Joey replied.

"Whatever, Joseph!"

"OK, I'm sorry. I shouldn't say that. I don't like it when people call me weird."

"People call you that?"

"Let's move on. We need to piece together things and see who else seems to show the symptoms Mr. Café was talking about. Think about Mom, Dad, Aunt Olivia, Grandma, all our friends at school —"

"Let's just relax," Ollie interrupted while putting a hand up.

"Ollie, nothing beats a failure but a try."

"OK, and when we get everyone to come together and figure out what their sixth sense is — then what do we do?"

"Then, God will smile at you and *you* will owe me a turkey sandwich," Joey said.

Joey and Ollie worked tirelessly on drawing their notes out.

"The main thing I'm stuck on is how our individual sixth senses help one another. They are so different!" Joey was scanning through all their notes. "Oh, and we need to add another thing.

"Oh, yeah?" Ollie replied, now tossing a ball in the air to keep awake.

"Yeah. Remember when we first saw the café?" Joey asked.

"Yes."

"You thought Mom had taken us there before, but I never remembered that. So, do you think you might have time jumped there before?"

"I don't think so, but I also don't know..." Ollie's voice drifted.

"Hmm, well, let's put a question mark by that. We've been at this for a while now. It's 4:47pm."

"Yeah, we could talk about this till the cows come home. I mean, all this probably doesn't amount to a hill of beans," Ollie said nonchalantly. Joey stared at Ollie blankly. Ollie shrugged, knowing he had said things he, himself, couldn't even comprehend, but was much too tired to care.

"Alright, well, let's think some more," Joey said as he put his sunglasses on.

"No, I'm hungry now." Ollie stood up, on his way to leave the room. As he did, the bedroom door swung open with their mother standing before them. Sapphire was in her arms.

"Boys, how's it going? I'm sorry we had to leave Grandma's so unexpectedly. Would you like to go get some ice cream?

"Sure!" they said in unison.

"Oh — will they have ice cream that doesn't have lactose in it?" Joey asked. Aria was both puzzled and impressed by her son's question.

"I'll call ahead and ask," she said, dialing the number as she walked away.

"Thanks," Ollie whispered.

"I told you I got your back," Joey said as he saw rays of green light shining everywhere.

A Baffling Dream With Ice Cream ⚇

"Pee-yew! Something's burning!" Joey exclaimed.

"You don't say pee-yew for a burning smell," Ollie replied.

"Then, what do you say for a burning smell, Oliver?"

"I honestly don't know."

"How sad."

"Yeah, you are," Ollie teased.

"I think you know what to say for a burning smell, and are just being cagey about it while we're stuck in here." Joey shook the metal bars in front of him.

"What does cagey mean? "Is it about being in a cage?" Ollie raised an eyebrow.

"I don't know — I guess! You're the wise one, remember?" Joey mocked.

"Well, you can't just make up words, Joey!"

"In my defense, I thought cagey was a real word — but if it isn't, why can't I make it up anyway? All words are made up, Ollie."

"True and honestly that word sounds kinda familiar." Ollie looked around the dark room they were in.

"It probably sounds familiar because we're literally stuck in a cage right now!" Joey exclaimed.

"Yeah — um, how exactly did we get inside here?" They both looked up at the ceiling lamp swaying back and forth across the way. It was the only thing in the room to look at.

"I'm just as confused as you," Joey replied.

"Well, so my last memory was — well, I don't even know!" Ollie cried.

"Why not — or are you just being cagey about things again?" Joey laughed.

"No, I really just can't remember!"

"You both know why you are here! You're here because your Dad didn't finish his business," a deep voice over an apparent hidden intercom announced.

"Oh, wow. That is completely disgusting! Why would Dad finishing his business on a toilet be of our concern?"

"Joey, I really don't think that's what he meant," Ollie said.

"Sir, just please get us out of here! I'm sure we can work something out! I'm good at a lot of stuff. I can walk your dog, cook you a turkey or grill you a plant-based burger as long as Mom watches me use the stove. Otherwise, I can have Ollie draw you some cool art!" While Joey was pleading for mercy, Ollie fidgeted with the bar locks, eventually breaking them, and welcoming their escape.

"Yes!" Ollie celebrated.

"Wow! You're magic!" Joey exclaimed.

"No, I'm wise — and stop being so loud. The speaker guy can clearly hear us. We need to figure out where we are and why. So, we need to be doing all that quietly." Joey nodded in response, and began helping his brother look around the dark, desolate warehouse they were in. Since they could hardly see anything, they had to touch, smell, and listen for any clues that could get them out. They tried opening every door they stumbled upon, but found that all were locked. The lamp's lightbulb began to flicker until eventually going out, leaving the boys in complete darkness.

"Did you see that door over there?" Joey asked.

"Over where, Joey? We are in the dark now."

"OK, then, we have to keep using senses other than sight to go and find that door!" Joey exclaimed.

"Fine. Oh, and not sure if it matters, but I feel like I've been here before," Ollie replied.

"Well, unless you being here before is going to help turn on the light and get us out of here, I suggest you follow my lead."

"I can't see you," Ollie said.

"I'll hold your hand."

"That's my foot!"

"Close enough," Joey replied, crawling them forward to an undisclosed location. "Wait! Let's go this way. Just keep hanging on!"

"How do you even know where you're going?" Ollie asked.

"Like I said, I'm using my other senses."

"Well, like *I* said, I feel like I've been here before," Ollie announced.

The boys felt the outlines of a small crawl space door that led them to the building's vents. As they crawled through, they smelled all kinds of aromas. Citrus scents filled the air, followed by smells of freshly baked breads and various meats cooking. They continued crawling through until they saw a bright light, which took them to a sight so spectacular, they were convinced their eyes were playing tricks on them. They found themselves standing in the middle of a lobby with décor so extravagant, you would have thought you were inside of a carnival. Hanging from the ceiling was a sign directing you to purchase anything from winter coats to gloves and scarves before entering into an ice cream cave. To the right of the sign, life-sized ice skaters glided to and fro. To the left, toy children were running, jumping, and throwing snow at one another. There were several kinds of other exaggerated scenes — including dancing snowmen hanging above their heads. Surprisingly, across the way, Ollie and Joey found their mother observing all of the scenery.

"Mom!" They both yelled as they ran up to her.

"Shh! You two should be observing the ambiance," she replied.

"What's that soap opera you watch, Aria? Is it called *The Old and the Restful* or *The Shy and the Ugly* or something like that?" Grandma Jade suddenly approached them.

"No, Mom, *I'm* the one who watches soap operas and that's not what either show is called," Aunt Olivia said as she walked up to join all of them.

"Stay out of this!" Grandma Jade snapped. "Anyway, that clutter of decorations over there — next to that other clutter of decorations — and to the right of that group of nutcrackers — reminds me of a scene from one of your soap opera episodes," she laughed. "The whole sight of that has me thinking of Joseph's room and how you allow him to mistreat it. Why don't you ever make him clean his property, Aria?"

"I do, Mom," Aria sighed.

"No, you don't. You give him the choice. That's the problem with your generation of parenting," Grandma Jade sighed.

"There are things you can learn from our age group too, Mom — especially the ones who are the aunts," Olivia cheerfully replied.

"Yeah, like what not to do," Grandma Jade rolled her eyes and picked up a peppermint stick. "All I'm saying is the building blocks you show them today are the soldiers they have for tomorrow."

"Well, I, for one, am a great role model for them. I exhibit independence, spontaneity, and flexibility," Olivia said, observing a holiday glass on sale.

"Can we please just stop talking and enjoy this?" Aria begged.

"Excuse me!" Joey exclaimed while bouncing up and down on his tippy-toes. "How did we all get in here?"

"Yeah, did you guys know we were trapped in a cage over there for almost forever?" Ollie exclaimed.

"Boys, what are you talking about?" Aria asked.

"They're probably just tired after watching this circus of delusion here. One can get rather overwhelmed by such tackiness," Grandma Jade said. "Not to mention, I bet their blood sugar levels are low. We need to get them some ice cream like you promised them."

"You boys ready? Put your coats on." Aria handed them their coats and directed them through a big, black iron door. The door led them to the inside of a cave where it was -7 degrees Celsius. Icicles were hanging from the ceiling inside of a large igloo-like bin that stood proudly in the middle of the room. They ooed and awed over the eleven rich and creamy tubs of frozen ice cream. The ice cream labels read, *Chocolate Chip Cookie Dough*, *Mint Chocolate Chip*, *Coffee Fix*, *Butter Pecan*, *Dulce de leche*, *Caramel Almond Brownie*, *Mango Love*, *Blueberry Dream*, *Trustworthy Taro*, and *Strawberry Castle*.

"Hi, I see the label for ten of these flavors, but what's the flavor of that beige one over there?" Aria asked the cashier.

"Ah, well, we call that flavor 'Red' even though the color's not exactly red," the skinny man behind the counter laughed. The lenses to his glasses were cloudy, so it was unclear if he was making eye contact with her as he spoke. "And since today is Black Friday, all of our flavors are half off. I definitely recommend you pay attention to all of our colors, especially the kind that's red."

"What did you just say?" Joey questioned.

"I said I definitely recommend all of our ice cream. It's an exceptionally new kind of spread."

"Oh, I heard something else," Joey said.

"Yeah, me too," Ollie replied.

"I didn't," Aria shrugged.

"Hey, you heard him say something about red, right?" Joey whispered to Ollie.

"Yeah, and why doesn't anyone realize or seem to care about us being locked in a cage?" Ollie asked.

"Yeah, and where is the speaker guy who was talking to us about Dad's unfinished toilet business?" Joey asked.

"This is all too crazy." Ollie began massaging his head.

"Maybe we're hallucinating and really just need some sugar like Grandma said," Joey sighed. As each one of them ordered their choice ice cream flavor, Joey scrunched his nose as he smelled a familiar burning smell. "Seriously, Ollie, what is that smell?"

"I don't smell anything. Anyway, should we go find Dad?" Ollie replied.

"Yeah. Hey, Mom, where's Dad?" Joey tugged on her shirt.

"Just eat your ice cream, dear," she replied.

"Seriously, Aria. When are you going to tell them?" Olivia muttered.

"When it's time. I don't want this leaking out and then they get ridiculed by people at school. They are at a prime age, Olivia," Aria said quietly.

"OK, so, since they have reached a prime age, as you say, knowing it all now is best. They'll also learn that the best weight to lose is the weight of other people's opinion," Olivia said.

"I know. I just don't think the world is ready for change."

"The only thing the world knows how to do is change! Those who resist change and throw all the fits in the world are still part of it. Listen, you can only control yourself. Plus, it's not like what you'll be explaining is a bad thing. The boys should learn that lesson today, not tomorrow."

"I know it isn't a bad thing, just not a popular one. Regardless, someone in the world will always try to make it be a bad thing."

"Stop caring about what the world deems as permissible, Aria! The media, themselves, would have nothing to report on if people weren't out there living!" Olivia cried.

"Well, I hope everyone is enjoying their ice cream. All of our flavors are organic, you know?" the cashier announced from afar.

"Why does he feel the need to speak to us when we've already paid him? Does he have nothing better to do?" Grandma Jade whispered.

"Mother, some people are happy with their jobs and actually like ensuring their customers are happy," Olivia replied.

"Well, Aria, you can go on and tell Justin that I'd be more suspicious of that man right there more than anything," Grandma Jade said sharply.

"Yes, we're fine," Aria said to the man before turning to her mother. "Why would Justin care?"

"What do you mean? You know why. He's learned the hard way of what it means to not pay attention and walk your destiny," Grandma Jade replied.

"Good — and all of our flavors are lactose-free," the man added.

"Well, that's important since I lack toast and tall mints," Ollie said cheerfully.

"No, you are lactos — nevermind." Joey shook his head. "Is your ice cream melting as fast as mine?" Joey asked, looking into Ollie's ice cream cup.

"Yeah, and it's freezing in here so that's weird." Ollie looked closely at Joey's ice cream cone.

"OK, boys, let's get out of this cold." Their mother hurried them toward the exit, when suddenly, a man opened the door. He was smiling so hard, his cheeks were rosy red. He was tall, muscular, and wearing a long, heavy trench coat. He had very fair skin, and a rather distinctive skinny mustache.

"You didn't think I'd let you leave, did you?" He stared at Aria intently. Aria's melting scoop of ice cream fell off its cone and onto the floor. The cashier saw the group encounter from afar, locked up the ice cream bin, and walked over to them.

"Poor Justin. He never truly tried so our bloodline easily won by a landslide," the cashier snickered.

"Who are you and what are you talking about?" Aria asked.

"Yeah, who are you — and I seriously thought Justin was fine!" Olivia snapped. The men ignored Olivia's interference and kept their eyes on Aria.

"Oh, we mean no harm or foul to you. We just wanted to stand here and thank Justin's crew. We are closing up this shop now anyway. It's half past our curfew. We have other invaluable appointments to attend to," the mustached man replied.

"As odd as it sounds, invaluable is a positive adjective — meant to compliment, so don't misconstrue," the cashier added.

"Thank you, my friend. That is rather true. Maybe we should just stand here and educate them — a consult will probably do. Yes, we shouldn't let you go just yet. Stay in this cool air and sit in your fright of us being here so out of the blue. I mean, it's as good a time as any for you to review the events of the past — a good ol' fashion generational rendezvous debut!"

"Yeah, and remember, doing anything to go against us now would just be tacky and taboo." Then, the men dramatically bowed as though they had just finished the performance of lifetime.

"Your rhyming was stupid!" Olivia yelled. During the whole performance, Joey saw beams of red around the two men. As they finished up their continuous bowing, the iron door swung open again. This time an angry looking Amber was in the doorway, ready to attack. She looked at Joey who nodded at her, which she took as her cue to pounce on the men with the strength of a rottweiler. She bit them from their shoulders to their ankles.

"OK, OK!" the cashier screamed.

"Yes, yes — you all can just go!" the mustached man cried. "It doesn't matter anyway. You already lost!" Despite their cries, Amber continued attacking them. Then, out of thin air, Olivia pulled out a red rope that securely tied them to one another. The iron door swung open once more, revealing five officers who waited for Grandma Jade's cue to take the men away. She nodded at them before flashing her badge at the men who were now wearing both red rope and handcuffs.

"God don't like ugly, and you two fools are some ugly acting people. Let me tell you somethin' — what's done in the dark will be seen in the light!" Grandma Jade preached. Ollie and Joey stood in disbelief, witnessing the whole event.

"Hey, did you have some secret conversation with Amber or something when she got here? It seemed like she was waiting on you to tell her she could attack," Ollie whispered to Joey.

"Yeah, I guess I did, but I don't get how that seemed so natural," Joey replied.

"Yeah, that's very crazy."

"Wait. Didn't Dad tell us a story about there being certain people animals listen to the most?"

"I don't remember — but it doesn't matter. Good job. I still feel like I've been here before. Like, this place doesn't necessarily look familiar, but it *feels* familiar." Ollie looked around while he walked with his family outside of the cave.

"So, everyone's OK, right?" Grandma Jade asked as she used her cane to close the iron door behind them. Amber wagged her tail and pawed at

Joey's leg. Joey picked her up and carried her to the parking lot they were walking to.

"Mom, who were those guys and why are they acting like you're their sheriff? I didn't even know you had Amber here! Oh, and Olivia, you just happened to have a thick red rope to tie those guys up with?" Aria squinted her eyes as she questioned them.

"Well, I can't speak for your sister, but I had a feeling. You can call me a worrywart all you want, but that feeling was the very reason none of you are hurt now! Plus, it proves Grandma Sheriff still got it!" Grandma Jade tossed her cane to the side and kicked one leg high in the air.

"Aria, just know this one's a sign for Justin," Olivia said as she helped herself to a big spoonful of ice cream from Ollie's cup.

"What do you mean?" Aria asked.

"Well, this should teach you to pay more attention to the energy around you. A person or a moment's energy tells you all you need to know." Olivia then began sampling the ice cream dripping from Joey's cone. "I mean, seriously, Aria — I'm giving you some mad wisdom here! I could very well be home, minding my own business, trying out this new hair style I've been wanting to model."

"Olivia, please! Alright now, Aria, as the parents, have you and Justin ever paid attention to your children?" Grandma Jade asked.

"Mom, I am really not in the headspace to receive a lecture right now." Aria began rubbing the back of her neck.

"No, I mean have you paid attention to Oliver's food sensitivities or to Joseph's connection to animals? You know you've been taught these signs before," Grandma Jade replied.

"Wait — when? Can we just talk about who those ice cream guys were before we continue a line of questioning?" Aria begged. "And, Olivia, why did you say this was a sign for Justin?"

"Because it is — and he needs to help teach Aria, as well."

"Why are you referring to me in the third person? I'm right here."

"You guys need to work together on this is all."

"Huh? So, since you're avoiding the elephant in the room, I'm assuming you two know who those two guys are."

"The only elephant here will be my behind if I don't get to my sunset hike," Grandma Jade replied.

"What? You don't hike. You don't even leave the house!" Aria cried.

"Listen, deep down, Justin truly understands this. He always has. I just wish he didn't miss his mark when he did. Then, you guys wouldn't have had to go through the trouble you did and Justin wouldn't be going through what he is now," Grandma Jade sighed. "I mean when he tried in the past and left, this all still made headlines."

"Wait, what? What made headlines?" Aria asked.

"Look, even though Justin's OK, he could be better. I mean, his story is still a good learning lesson to tell people. It'll be good for the boys if they knew the whole story. That's all I'm saying." Olivia began looking for her car keys.

"Aria, sometimes your unfinished business signals you in ways you'll pay attention to the most. Sometimes the weirder your signal seems, the more off your path you are. Just get back on your destiny and at least support the boys through theirs," Grandma Jade said as she opened the car door.

"Oh, speaking of destiny, can we play 'Destiny's Child' on the way back, Mom? I'm in the mood for a throwback. You catch my drift?" Olivia began dancing.

"Child, let's get warmed up before the thing we catch is a cold before I'm ready for my hike," Grandma Jade replied.

"Wow, OK. So, I guess that's it?" Aria tried getting their attention, but knew she failed when the car reversed out of its parking space.

"I mean, what more is there to say?" Grandma Jade called from out of the window. As Aria turned to face her kids, she slipped on one of the many puddles of ice cream on the ground. As she tried to get up, she heard a voice calling her husband's name.

"Justin....Justin!" Aria was hovering over her husband. She was dabbing a wet washcloth across his forehead. "You're talking a lot in your sleep again." Justin put his hand to his head.

"Um, what time is it?" he asked, looking at the clock which read 4:48pm. "And what day is it?"

"Same day you fell asleep in — Friday — *Black* Friday. You have been sleeping through all the major retail deals. Ehh, it's a scam anyway."

"But where's your mother and Amber?"

"They should be home. She hardly leaves the house, and when she does, I doubt she'd take Amber."

"And where's your sister?"

"At her house, I assume," Aria said.

"And where are the boys?"

"Well, I just came from their rooms."

"So, they aren't locked in a cage or anything, right?"

"What's wrong with you?"

"Aria, I think you were right. It is all happening again — and I'm getting all these signs to stop suppressing it. With all my sleep-talking, my sleep-walking and now this dream..."

"What happened in this dream?"

"First, I saw things from the boys' perspective for some reason. They had also given themselves nicknames, by the way."

"Yeah? What were they?"

"Ollie and Joey."

"Hmm, not bad," she nodded.

"Yeah, and then the dream switched to me seeing things through your eyes I think," Justin said slowly.

"Yeah? Well, the Bible says we become one when we get married, so that's not shocking," Aria replied.

"Yeah, but it kind of kept going back and forth between the boys' perspective and yours — or mine?"

"Huh?"

"Listen, do you think I kept getting changes in perspective so I'd pay attention to the dream more?"

"I don't know, Justin. You're the expert for things like this. Did you ever study this upon becoming a therapist?"

"Even though I'm a professional, I'd still like to talk it out."

"You're right. I digress, but I really think this is just your cold talking. I mean, that's why we left my mother's house early, remember? You got that call, fell asleep during that call, and thought you must have been falling under the weather."

"No, that's what you chose to believe. I told you what I thought." Justin reached for his glass of water.

"Yeah, you're right. You did." Aria looked down at her shoes. "So, these magical energies you think you possess or, excuse me, these postmonitions you say you're getting are nothing more than dreams, right? I mean, I'm sorry, but I lock people up who talk like this!"

"Stop it, Aria," Justin snapped.

"Sorry, sorry — and why are you holding your head like that?" she asked.

"It just hurts. I fell — or you fell — in my dream, and it still hurts." Just then, there was a knock on their slightly ajar bedroom door.

"Mom, Dad," can we go see Mr. Café?" Joey asked with Ollie standing close behind him.

"No, your Dad's not feeling well and I need to stay home with him."

"No, go ahead," Justin replied.

"They've been there twice in the past forty-eight hours, Justin! Any more time with him and we'll be ordered to pay child support!"

"Pleeeease," Joey begged.

"Fine, I'll take you. Go get in the car — and be sure to give him money no matter what you do or do not order. He wouldn't take the money I tried giving him the other day," she muttered, reaching into her purse and handing Joey a $20 bill.

"Thanks! We'll meet you in the car!" Joey exclaimed. As the boys dashed out, Justin looked closely at Aria.

"OK, so you can go over more details about your dream when I get back."

"OK, but before you go, answer me something."

"Yes?" Aria asked

"Was Oliver standing behind Joseph completely asleep just now?"

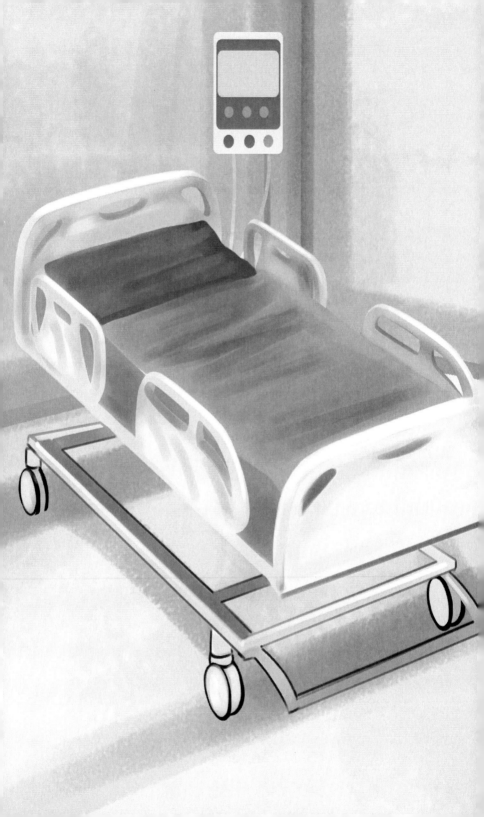

A Healing Talk With Mr. Finny ♉

The boys arrived at the café to find two other tables being waited on by a man who reminded them of Mr. Café. Ollie and Joey went to the same table they sat at the last time. The man was wearing a dull expression as he approached their table.

"Got your parents here?" he asked.

"No, sir, but is Mr. Café here?" Joey asked.

"Uh, who? I'm Mr. Cowfinaé," he replied.

"I thought Mr. Café had that as his real last name too," Ollie said.

"Well, no problem. We can call you Mr. Finny," Joey said proudly.

"Sure, I've been called worse." The man shrugged his shoulders and scribbled something into his notepad.

"So, are you and Mr. Café brothers or something?" Ollie asked.

"Are me and mister who brothers?" The boys stared at one another, not knowing how else to rephrase their question. "Nah, I'm just pulling your leg. I get that you must have a nickname thing with him going on — even though neither of your names are Nick, right?" he laughed.

"No!" Ollie smiled wide.

"You guys are funny! Well, anyway, my brother is home with his grandson today," Mr. Finny said.

"So, cool. Mr. Café is your brother!" Ollie exclaimed.

"He's my younger brother. Since I'm the oldest, I'm naturally the wiser one. Don't tell him I said that."

"Why? I believe he should know the truth," Joey said.

"He'd battle me in a relay race of some sort to prove otherwise. Anyway, what did you all need?" Mr. Finny asked.

"Well, um, you see, Mr. Café — he had..." Joey searched for the words to make a complete sentence.

"You must have questions from something he talked to you about," Mr. Finny replied. "Well, let me go tend to those other two tables over there and I'll be back in a jiffy." Mr. Finny left the boys sitting in their confusion.

"OK — why do he and Mr. Café say jiffy? Is that a peanut butter joke or something?" Ollie's eyes were glued to Mr. Finny catering to the tables across the way.

"It's probably just an old person joke or something. He's a grown up. Grown ups make lame, old person jokes."

"Yeah, I guess no grown up is really all that funny," Ollie sighed.

"Yeah, you should know. You act like a grown up sometimes," Joey replied.

"You may think I'm acting like a grown up when all I'm doing is acting with common sense!"

"Nevertheless, you act old!"

"No, I act with wisdom!" Ollie replied.

"Point is, you're not that funny."

"Point is, we need to get back on track."

"Right. We have a lot of work to do, but since Mr. Café isn't here, we aren't going to make progress today. We'll need to take some time to rethink things," Joey proclaimed.

"Why do you feel the only help we can get is from Mr. Café?" Ollie asked.

"I don't know. Just 'cause." Joey turned away and shrugged his shoulders.

"Well, can you at least take those glasses off? We're inside and you wearing them inside is distracting me."

"Then, don't look at me, alright? Good. I'm happy to have solved your problem right there," Joey replied as he looked for anything that resembled a mirror so he could look at himself.

"I can take a picture of you wearing them. It'll last longer," Ollie said, rolling his eyes.

"Alright, listen, with or without these sunglasses on, I have the ability to see colors and numbers, and taste and smell things that remind me of stuff, right? Well, that doesn't matter because I like wearing these. They are my training wheels that help me see it all much easier. OK? Whatever. I'll take them off." Joey folded his sunglasses up and set them on the table.

"Listen, if you keep doing what's comfortable, you'll never learn," Ollie replied.

"I don't know what you mean."

"You said you can see color and stuff without wearing your glasses, so you gotta teach yourself to connect the numbers and smells and stuff on your own — whether you have your glasses on or not. That way, you'll always stay aware."

"Well, Ollie, for once, you actually make sense."

"Eh, I make dollars — but anyway, what about my sixth sense?" Ollie bounced in his seat, eager to redirect the conversation.

"Ok, well, I think you have to pay attention while you're in your dreams more. Like, I know you told me what happened in them, but I think you need to *do* more while you're in them. That way, you'll figure out the hidden meaning of things. Like, you should talk to people you see there, or explore outside of that house you said you had taken a bath in."

"Yeah, it was really weird being asked to take a bath in a kitchen."

"Well, like Dad always says, I'm sure stranger things have happened," Joey replied.

"That was strange enough. Anyway, I'm too scared to even be in that place. I don't think I could leave that apartment and go explore! So, let's just go over how my gifts from Mr. Café connect to the dreams I'm having. Like, what am I supposed to do with a watch and socks other than wear them?"

"Well, try playing with the buttons on your watch or something — and for the socks, well, think about what the purpose of socks normally are."

"The purpose is to wear them, Joseph." Ollie rolled his eyes and shook his head.

"Well, I mean, socks also keep your feet warm and clean, right? I don't know — just think like that."

"Alright," Ollie sighed.

"And remember you gotta give me more to write about in my notebook, so you gotta *do* more in those dreams, Oliver! It's honestly probably the only way we'll be able to connect our abilities to one another."

"I hear you, Joseph."

"Just try to talk to people more in your dreams. Like you were telling me, take those training wheels off and put effort into your dreams. You should trust me anyway, Oliver. I'm older. I've had a lot more experiences with effort in my years. Effort is the thing that raised my science grade up to the 'D' it deserved."

"Alright, well, let's move on and think what the dog treats from Mr. Café may have been about" Ollie closed his eyes tightly, hoping it would help him think better.

"I don't know much else other than it being what it was. They were treats for a dog. Although, when Jasper spoke to me, it was, in fact, the same night I gave out the treats. I don't know if him talking has to do with the treats though because when I tried talking to Sapphire the next morning, she wouldn't speak to me."

"Maybe she was busy or this has nothing to do with the treats."

"Well, I even tried talking to Amber when we were at Grandma's house, but she wouldn't speak to me either."

"Maybe she doesn't like you anymore," Ollie chuckled. Just then, Mr. Finny walked over and switched out the wobbly chair seated at their table with a chair that was more stable.

"So, what questions do you have now?" he asked as he sat down.

"I mean, well, Mr. Café gave us these gifts that we're trying to figure out the meaning of or use for," Joey said.

"And?" Mr. Finny raised an eyebrow.

"And we're confused about them all," Ollie said.

"Well, you've been on the right track for the last couple of minutes about some things." Mr. Finny leaned back in his chair.

"Wait. You could hear us from all the way over there?" Joey's eyes grew wide.

"Go back to your analysis on the socks," Mr. Finny instructed. "What purpose do socks have?"

"Their purpose is to keep you warm and clean," Ollie said proudly.

"Yes, now go deeper than that. They're underlying purpose is to keep you…"

"Really warm!" Ollie exclaimed.

"When you wear socks, what are they directly touching?"

"My feet," Ollie replied.

"And?"

"I don't know."

"The ground, my dear boy. The socks are your reminders to stay grounded. So, I take it you suffer from sleep-talking or sleep paralysis, right?"

"Yes," Ollie nodded while his cheeks turned rosy red.

"Try resting with your socks on. Maybe it'll remind you to stay grounded and confident in whatever moment you're dreaming of. Then, you'll be that much closer to uncovering why you chose to dream of that moment," Mr. Finny replied.

"But I never choose! They're just dreams! Dreams aren't real!" Ollie exclaimed.

"They aren't?" Mr. Finny raised an eyebrow.

"Plus, I'm not sure my socks can come with me in my dreams."

"I guess you'll have to make sure they do," Mr. Finny replied. "And a word from the wise here, sleep paralysis is just your spirit leaving your body. It'll come back. Just be calm and allow it to. You haven't been grounded enough in your dreams yet. That's why your spirit has had trouble finding its way back to you. With training, however, you'll grasp that ability."

"You seriously think I have control over my dreams and stuff that happens to me?" Ollie asked.

"I think you have more control over things than you're taught you do. If you forget everything, remember this — those dreams you have certainly aren't random. *You* choose where to go and *you* choose when to go to it. You're not just simply dreaming." Mr. Finny stood up from the table.

"Now, you two — and whoever else you find using more than ten percent of their brain — should start paying attention to sixth sense abilities more. We need to be applying them to help the life we have here. People who complain about being bored all the time aren't using their brains at all. They surely aren't living life the way it's intended to be lived — and if you ever complain you're bored, then it's your fault for actually being too lazy to get up and learn something. There's a lot to do to improve this world, ya know?" The boys looked at one another confused. "I'm not going to say another word. It'll just confuse you. Now, you should go ahead and wake up."

"What?" Ollie raised his eyebrow.

"Well, you're still dreaming," Mr. Finny replied. Suddenly, Ollie woke up in a hospital bed with IV fluids hooked up to his hands, arms, and legs. Joey was by his side, viciously scribbling in his notebook.

"Dude, you finally woke up! No need to tell me a thing! I wrote it all down here. You talked *a lot* in that dream! My only question is — is Mr. Finny real?"

"What?" Ollie put his hand to his head. "Why am I in a hospital? Where is Mom?"

"She's in the cafeteria with Dad getting us dinner. You fell asleep and wouldn't wake up, so Mom freaked out and rushed you to the hospital."

"I thought we were on our way to get ice cream," Ollie said while rubbing his eyes.

"Ice cream? Oh, I forgot all about that, but yeah, after you said something about cows coming home and then something about beans, you knocked out on my rug. I managed to wake you up — and you stayed awake long enough for us to go ask Mom and Dad if we could go to the café, but then you fell asleep again and we couldn't wake you."

"What? No, no! Mom came into your room and asked us if we wanted ice cream and then we all left to go eat it!" Ollie cried.

"Dude, you must have been dreaming longer than you think — or at least definitely longer than you talked out loud about because all I have here are notes about Mr. Finny."

"Really?"

"Anyway, like I was saying, we were leaving the house so we could go to the café, but then you fell asleep while we were walking in the house and stuff I guess."

"Wait. Are you sure?" Ollie sat up in his hospital bed.

"Seriously, Ollie. How do you fall asleep while already awake and walking? I mean, at least

Dad's already asleep when he begins walking around! Anyway, things worked out for me because Mom let me eat your leftover turkey while we were on our way to the hospital." Joey began smacking his lips.

"Well, maybe all of this was meant to happen so I could help us answer a lot of the questions we have."

"Oh, yeah! All the talking you always like to do finally paid off!"

"All of *my* talking? You're the talker!"

"I control myself enough to only talk while I'm awake." Joey laughed as he reviewed the notes in his notebook. "So, let's digest. I think if you go back to sleep, we can figure out everything else and we'll be done with this whole confusing puzzle of sixth senses! I can't wait to be done with training! I mean, we basically are already done!"

"You think it's just that easy?"

"I think it just might be! On that note, I don't mind punching you in the face so you knock out and go back to sleep," Joey suggested.

"Seriously, if our abilities are meant to connect to one another, I don't think it's as simple as me going back to sleep and waking up with answers for us."

"Yeah, maybe you're right." Joey put his pen down.

"Yeah, Rome wasn't built in a day."

"There you go again. You have such weird phrases that don't even sound like they're from this generation!" Joey threw his hands in the air.

"Wait. That must be it!" Ollie exclaimed.

"What?"

"What did Mr. Finny say in my dream? He said I wasn't ever *simply* dreaming! He said there is a reason I choose to go to the places I do! Maybe my dreams are more memories! Maybe I lived in that time before and want to be back there for some reason." Ollie was now smiling from ear to ear, as though he cracked The Vernam Cipher.

"But, then again, maybe that dream was just a dream. Maybe it was all just you talking in your sleep," Joey sighed.

"At this point, things are 50/50," Ollie said.

"OK, fine, I won't doubt it. I'll play along." Joey tapped his pen on Ollie's hospital bed as he pondered. "So, if what you said in your dream really is the direction we need to go, I wonder if —"

"If I can take you with me?" Ollie asked.

"There's your second sixth sense," Joey said. "You can read my mind."

A Christmas Eve Journey ♋

Twenty-eight days had passed and everyone had gone back to their normal lives. Justin forgot to make dinner approximately twenty-four times, Aria spent about fourteen days shopping for different flavored coffees, Ollie and Joey went to school and back home without any desire to visit the café. No dreams of the past, sight of color, or talking dogs took place for almost a month. This was most likely because their mother kept them on a tight leash and on an even tighter routine after Ollie's hospital scare.

It was now the day before Christmas, and school was out for the boys again. Ollie and Joey sat at the kitchen table in deep conversation as Aria prepared dinner.

"You smell how good those cookies are?" Joey asked.

"Yeah, I want ALL of them!" Ollie replied with eyes opened wide. "But Mom said not until after we eat dinner."

"Don't be scared. Just take it. She's not even looking!"

"I can't. I don't want to be too full for dinner!"

"When you get older, you'll understand, but I will say, you sound like a baby right now," Joey replied.

"I'm not though."

"Then, just take the cookie," Joey shrugged.

"No," Ollie said, crossing his arms.

"Why?"

"Because," Ollie replied.

"Ugh, because why, Ollie?"

"Because I don't want to anymore! I've grown past even wanting it!"

"You are a wimp," Joey teased.

"That's your opinion — and anyway, I'm still clearly wiser than you."

"Well, that's your opinion."

"Not really. You prove it to be a fact every day," Ollie said.

"Well, I took a cookie. Now, you should."

"Yeah, well, I don't think that's how it works."

"Listen, Ollie, I'm preparing you for life. I'm trying to teach you things."

"Teachings happen in school," Ollie replied.

"Oliver, life starts outside of school. School is just your training wheels. So, I'm truly here to let you know that if you don't take the cookie, you'll turn poor."

"How does that even make sense?" Ollie asked.

"When you and I are the same age, then you'll understand," Joey replied.

"You are seriously…"

"Seriously what?" Joey asked.

"Just seriously less than smart," Ollie replied. "And, by the way, we'll never be the same age at the same time."

"Then, I guess you'll never really understand."

"Leave me alone!" Ollie turned away.

"OK, then. You obviously want to turn poor."

"Well, I believe poor is just a mindset," Ollie sighed.

"Fine — learn the hard way."

"Are you stupid or just pretending to be because you make no sense!" Ollie cried.

"But do I make dollars? "Joey teased.

"Stop stealing my come-backs!"

"Then, take the cookie!" Joey yelled.

"Fine — if it'll make you stop talking!" Ollie cried.

"What? You've lost your willpower now or something?"

"You literally just told me to —"

"Listen, I just want you to do better in life."

"And I just want this conversation to be over." Ollie slowly bit into a cookie.

"Oliver, spit that out," Aria sang while subtly dancing. Since Aria had her headphones on and her back turned to them, the boys thought their conversation was private.

"How did you even know, Mom?" Ollie asked as crumbs fell from his mouth.

"I have a sixth sense," Aria smiled.

"Aria, I'm finally done!" Justin said, bursting through the kitchen. "Oh and you made cookies!"

"Touch that and it'll be your hand," Aria warned.

"But it's been a long day," Justin whined.

"It's been a longer one for me — and I am doing *your* dinner duties. Please never overbook your day again. Your long hours stress me out."

"Uh, pot — black!" Justin chuckled as he bit into a cookie.

"Good job, Dad. We won't turn poor now," Ollie said from across the way.

"Don't listen to him, Dad. Kids these days make nonsense things up. Am I right?" Joey replied.

"Justin, I am not the pot calling the kettle black. I am *Mrs. Black* who is exhausted from Mr. Black's sleep-walking every night."

"Or you're tired from your long work hours." Justin happily licked the melted chocolate chips off his fingers. Aria stopped slicing the vegetables she was cutting, took her headphones off, placed her hands on her hips, and stared deep into her husband's eyes. She hoped this nonverbal communication would be enough for her husband to say something more pleasant. "Yes, yes. I know. I told you — I'll figure my sleep-walking, talking, and all that out!" He smiled as he took a napkin and grabbed another cookie that was still steaming on the cookie sheet.

"It's just that you spend several weeks *not* figuring it out, Justin. I just…" she tried to find the words.

"OK, go sit down. I'll take over dinner. Thank you for starting it."

"The food is already plated. I was just cutting these carrots up for us to have on the side."

"Those aren't carrots, Aria," Justin replied.

"What do you mean?" she asked holding one closer to her face.

"I mean, those aren't carrots," he repeated. "They're parsnips."

"OK, well they're the same shape and color as carrots, Justin."

"No, they aren't. I mean, they're the same shape, yes, but not the same color."

"Huh?" Aria stared closer.

"Go lay down, dear. I think you overwhelmed yourself with Christmas shopping with your mother."

"You're probably right. Oh, that reminds me — she got me a sort of coffee of the month basket for Christmas."

"What? She already told you what she got you? She couldn't wait for tomorrow?"

"She knew I was about to buy it, so she folded."

"What a great poker player," Justin teased. "Anyway, I made a gingerbread house for human consumption."

"I thought that was only a Thanksgiving thing, strictly for dog consumption."

"Well, now I'm starting a new tradition for us humans for Christmas. I mean, you gotta do something different with your pumpkin if you want the spice to live on and prosper."

"Was that a pumpkin spice latte joke?" Aria asked.

"Yes — 'Tis the season for me." Justin began collecting the dinner plates to bring to the table.

"The kids are right — we aren't funny." They both laughed. "You know, we can go to that café the boys like and get lattes before we schlep to my mother's tonight," Aria replied.

"Alright! Done — like butter!" Justin exclaimed.

"What does 'done like butter' even mean?"

"It's my way of being in the utmost agreement with you." They both looked at the boys across the way. "Yeah, we really aren't funny. Anyway, I'll pack the boys up after dinner." Aria watched Justin serve the plates to Ollie and Joey.

"Yep, cheers to our dinner here with apparent parsnips on the side," she giggled.

At the café, the boys noticed their favorite table being used by a baby blowing bubbles into his frozen hot chocolate, a girl eating an oreo brownie sundae bigger than her head, and their parents sampling one another's croissants and hot drinks using the tiniest utensils. All the tables were packed. In fact, the entire place was packed, causing Ollie and Joey to stand shoulder to shoulder. Mr. Café was nowhere in sight, but they saw many servers running to and fro, trying their best to serve everyone as quickly as possible. Despite the chatter inside, you could hear the Christmas music playing, and watch the fireplace flames dancing to every beat. The café was decorated with Christmas cheer. There were nutcrackers in each corner of the room, a section of ballerinas dancing various numbers,

Santa Clauses of every ethnicity on display with Jesus, angels, and the Christian cross center stage. There were green and white Christmas trees, reindeer with long, artistic antlers, gifts that lit up anytime someone walked by. Many children enjoyed observing the toy dog playing tug-of-war with the toy elf over in a corner.

"This line is outrageous!" Justin cried.

"Well, we don't have work tomorrow so we have the time," Aria shrugged.

"Well, I'm here for someone to WOW me with their notorious pumpkin spice latte creation!" he yelled, hoping it would encourage someone to serve them faster.

"You know, usually people who love sweet potato pie don't like anything pumpkin," Aria laughed.

"Well, you know I am a rare breed," Justin replied.

"Yes, to put it lightly," Aria nodded.

"Oh! You're Ollie and Joey's parents!" Mr. Café exclaimed, holding a tray full of desserts.

"Hi, Mr. Café! The boys are somewhere around here." Aria looked around as she spoke. "But this is my husband —"

"Yes, Justin. We've met," Mr. Café said with a pleasant smile while a crowd gathered around him to take the dessert-filled sample cups from his tray.

"Tell the boys to enjoy the joy of this place tonight!" Mr. Café yelled while the crowd was swallowing him whole.

"So, you two already met?" Aria looked intently at her husband.

"I have never seen that man a day in my life," Justin replied.

The boys were playing a game on the floor of the café. They crawled over people's feet, slid under chairs, and tried seeing how fast they could make it to the other side of the café without touching anything along the way. When they reached the other side, they were surprised to see a small door they could crawl through. As they crawled, they found themselves in a dark tunnel. It smelled of sweet cinnamon sugar they assumed to be the array of pastries baking in the kitchen behind them. As they continued moving, the aroma transitioned into the smell of freshly baked bread. Then, they took a deep breath and smelled apple pie. Although it was rather dark where they were, the smells of baked goods carried on until they reached a light that took them to an area they were able to stand straight up in. The area was as blank as printer paper. Other than themselves, they couldn't see, smell, or hear anything. Suddenly, a sign appeared in front of them that read *Left or Right*. The boys stared at it and looked around. They hoped something else would appear that would help them make sense of it all.

"But there aren't any doors," Ollie finally said. "So, how are we supposed to go left or right?"

"I know. This is either really cool or really weird," Joey replied. "This isn't one of your dreams you finally pulled me into, is it?" Joey smiled while trying to contain his excitement.

"I don't think so..." Ollie said slowly.

"So, what are we supposed to do?"

"Why are you asking me? You're older!"

"And you're wiser!" Joey looked up then back down at the sign. "But let's take one thing at a time. So, where do we want to go — left or right?" Ollie shrugged his shoulders in response. The boys continued staring at the sign, hoping it would make the decision for them.

"I mean, so, what exactly comes with going left versus going right?" Ollie asked.

"See, that's part of your problem, Ollie. Sometimes you just have to make a decision and take the risks that come along with it," Joey said as he stood up tall.

"Very good." A man with a beaming British accent replied as he approached them out of nowhere. It was Mr. Finny!

"Wait! I thought I just made you up!" Ollie gasped. "I wasn't positive you were real!"

"Well, yes, and no," Mr. Finny replied. "I mean, I'm real but my sixth sense — or part of it anyway — is an interesting one. OK, well, we did previously meet and —"

"Huh?" Ollie scratched his head.

"OK, you see, my sixth sense is as follows: I can lucid dream. I can dream about bouncing a basketball. Then, I can wake up and see that very basketball. I, unsurprisingly, found this out years after suffering from sleep paralysis — but then again, that was part of my past life regression. Anyway, I'm rambling. The bottom line is, at some point, you and I were experiencing sleep paralysis at the same time and our spirits met. Sleep paralysis happens when your spirit leaves your body to explore. Now, whatever your spirit is exploring is your business. However, at some point, you found it necessary to find my spirit to help make sense of it all." The boys stared at him blankly.

"So, what and who can we trust? How do we know a dream from reality? Like, are you and Mr. Café even really brothers?" Joey asked.

"My good fellow, does that really matter? Use your oxygen to ask questions that progress you forward in life," he smiled.

"But, you see, we don't know what things to ask to move forward!" Joey cried.

"Well, you were giving your brother very good advice just now. Remember, we all need each other. I take it you both have different sixth senses, right? So, you are both going to need to do simultaneous work during your training."

"How do we find the training?" Ollie asked.

"You already found it," he replied, "And you did a good job at finding me while you dreamt, Ollie. Many can't do that — even more won't do it." Mr. Finny began looking around the blank room they were standing in.

"We need to get back on track. There are absolutely no doors here," Joey whined and kicked the air in front of him.

"Well, if you want something in life, you need to look for it. God will help you along the way," Mr. Finny nodded.

"You seem very different than in my dream," Ollie replied.

"Yeah, well, you know — I'm trying to do keto for two weeks." Mr. Finny pulled up his trousers.

"No, I mean, your personality," Ollie replied.

"Oh, well, yes, I'm British and not as blunt or as rough around the edges as you comprehended me to be in our spirit-world encounter."

"How and why did I create you like that then? It's honestly interesting you even know I created you like that in the first place!"

"All you need to know is you apparently saw and created what helped you and your brother understand. My spirit simply helped your spirit. You'll find similar instances of this as you go on and grow. Although, be careful while you do. You don't want to make false-positives about a person or a situation. Doing so can quickly get you off your path, OK? Alright! So, it was nice catching up. See you both when I see you." Instead of walking away like the boys anticipated, Mr. Finny stood in place.

"Aren't you leaving?" Joey asked.

"No, you are." He pointed at the above sign that read, *Left or Right*.

"Well, I need to work on being ambidextrous, so let's go right," Joey said.

"Uh-uh. If I need to work on being that too, we need to go left!" Ollie snapped.

"Well, do we need to go the same way?"

"Well, what if I get lost?"

"Then, figure out how to get found."

"That was deep, but Joey, what should we do? I don't want us to choose the wrong way."

"Remember that whole taking risks thing I was telling you about?" Ollie knew his brother was right. He generally couldn't help but be fearful when it came to making decisions like this. Joey was equally afraid, but didn't want to show it. Joey was secretly hoping exhibiting bravery would help his little brother find courage.

"OK, well, I would like to go left, and you gotta come with me," Ollie nodded.

"Alright," Joey nodded back. Suddenly, the room shook. Ollie and Joey hugged one another, trembling in fear. A strong wind entered, rippling their cheeks.

"What's happening?" Ollie cried.

"I don't know!" Joey yelled. Then, Joey's jaw dropped. He couldn't believe his eyes. He was walking on the same sidewalk he and his brother were on when they first saw the café in the distance. The difference now was Joey was alone and saw colors and numbers boldly around him. He saw them hovering over both nature and city objects. He then heard Aunt Olivia's voice, but it was quickly drowned out by the smell and sight of cookies sitting on a plate on his kitchen counter. As he reached for one, the scene around him changed to him standing in front of Ollie's bedroom door after having gotten kicked out of it Thanksgiving morning. Joey then felt something furry tickle his ankle. He looked down and saw Amber brushing up against him.

"Are you ready?" she asked.

"I don't think I have time not to be, right?" Joey replied. Then, Sapphire appeared and used her nose to slide Joey's sunglasses to him.

"Do you want to try wearing these or would you like to continue without them?" she asked.

"What's the best option?" Joey raised his eyebrow.

"Whichever option you choose, it's your risk to take," she replied.

"Yeah, just like you tell Ollie, how you respond to everything is all on you," Jasper said, suddenly appearing before him.

"So, just confirm for me — I'm clearly a dog whisperer, right?" Joey asked.

"Oh, can I tell him? Can I? Can I?" Sapphire bounced up and down.

"Go ahead," Jasper replied.

"OK, so, you can speak to any animal you earn the trust with. So, just remember, the lower they lay, the greater things they have to say," she replied. Then, just like that, the three dogs disappeared. As Joey was experiencing all of this, Ollie was seeing visuals of his past time neighborhood. He saw many things around him he did not recognize. Suddenly, a stranger gave him two cloth bags filled with food. Ollie looked to the side of him and saw a woman he had dreamt of before. She was rushing down the apartment steps with a lamp in her hand. His surroundings then transitioned into watching himself sleep. He was petrified, watching his spirit lift up from his body. It then began to wander around before moving at the speed of both light and sound. He managed to follow his spirit through what looked to be outer space. He didn't realize he somehow morphed into being the spirit himself. There wasn't much around him but balls of light. While he moved, he felt completely out of control. He consistently bumped into anything he passed. Whenever he collided with a ball of light, it would poof into a full bodied, human-like ghost he was able to make eye contact with.

"Excuse me!" Ollie cried as he competed in a marathon he hoped would at least give him a medal in the end.

"Watch out!" one snapped.

"Hey, did you hear? Garrett Morgan invented the traffic light! I just read about it in the paper!" another exclaimed.

"Slow down!" one demanded.

"Sweetie, did you forget again?" one asked.

"Hey, watch it!" another scolded.

"Did you want to go to a drive-in movie?" one asked.

"Excuse you!" one scoffed.

"Hey, Marilyn Monroe came out with a new

picture," another said.

"Did you hear Martin Luther King Jr.'s 'I Have A Dream' speech? He just did it today!" one proclaimed.

"That new Motown music label you were telling me about — do you have any of the records?" another asked.

"Hey! That Jackson 5 group is playing live at the music hall. Will you go with me?" another pleaded.

"Will you just slow down?" one barked.

"Walt Disney World just opened up and we're going on a family trip. Pack your bags!" another exclaimed.

"Aye, there's a station on television supporting black people — not joking! It seriously just came out! It's called 'BET.' It's going to pave the way and show our people's story!" another announced. Suddenly, everything went dark. Ollie blinked his eyes and he was next to Joey sitting behind steering wheels and several buttons.

"Um, did you just see a bunch of..." Ollie tried to find the words to finish his sentence.

"Yeah," Joey replied, equally flabbergasted. "But this is all so cool!"

"Welcome gentlemen," Mr. Café said, appearing before them on a large screen. "This is your introductory training course. During your training — time, as you know it, stands still, so Mom and Dad won't think but five minutes have passed. No one told you to be here. You found it on your own — remember that. You mustn't be too long though. Santa is on his way tonight." Then, the screen powered itself off.

"Wait. We got literally no instructions!" Joey exclaimed.

"Well, it's settled. Mr. Café is magic," Ollie sighed.

"He said our powers — or our abilities, our sixth sense or whatever isn't magic!" Joey yelled. Ollie shrugged and started looking around. Behind them was a transparent refrigerator and bar stocked with food. As the boys walked further back, they saw a bathroom that had a walk-in shower, a jetted tub, a toilet with different colors of water inside of it, and a sink that talked to them. When they finished their tour of what appeared to be the coolest submarine in the world, they walked back to find a man behind the bar.

"Welcome!" the man said. "I'm Mr. Tender." The boys smiled and waved at him, trying to mask their fear. "What can I quench your thirst with before you start your training?"

"Um, we can't have alcohol," Joey said.

"Why, 'Tis true, sir, but this here is a bar full of juices, milk, and smoothies of your choice.

Alcohol does nothing but cause you to make an array of bad decisions anyway. Keep that in mind. So, anyway, what'll it be?"

"Do you have a mango smoothie?" Ollie asked.

"Do you have an açaí one?" Joey bounced up and down.

"Of course!" Mr. Tender proclaimed. He gathered fresh fruit, two decadent cups and straws. "So, what are your names?"

"I'm Joey and this is my younger brother Ollie," Joey replied.

"Yeah, but I'm the wiser one," Ollie announced.

"Joseph and Oliver. You have profound names," Mr. Tender said as he watched the blender silently blend.

"What's profound about it?" Joey asked.

"Well, it's really what you make it to be — less than what society tells you it is." The boys stared at him blankly. "Your names are even more profound when they're written out." He snapped his fingers and the two straws he had changed their shape into spelling out the boys' names before diving inside their two empty smoothie cups. "Even more profound now, isn't it?" Mr. Tender laughed as he threw a towel over his shoulder.

"So, what is all of this?" Joey gestured around him.

"It's what you make it," Mr. Tender replied.

"Is anyone ever going to give us a straight answer?" Joey sighed.

"It's your life! Do the best you can with it," Mr. Tender said, filling their cups. "Alright, these should be some good and organic fuel for you two. I hope they taste good!"

"Delicious!" they both said after one sip. The ingredients Mr. Tender had taken out jumped for joy before putting themselves away. The boys were dumbfounded.

"Mom said we had to leave money when people give us stuff." Joey blew off a piece of lent from the penny he found in his pocket before handing it to Mr. Tender.

"Not for me." Mr. Tender put one hand up.

"OK. So, do you do this all the time?" Joey asked.

"Do what?" Mr. Tender asked, wiping the countertop.

"He means do you stay under water in a submarine and make magical smoothie drinks," Ollie said.

"Oh, well, only when someone's here," he said.

"Wait, so are you...?" Joey squinted at him.

"I'm a robot," Mr. Tender nodded. "Part of why money has no value to me. Funny though — if only humans could wrap their heads around that same concept, there'd be so much less trouble in the world. There would be a lot more laughter and joy."

"OK, well, thanks, Mr. T! We're excited and want to go get started!" Joey slurped the last of his drink and jumped out of his seat.

"We love you, Mr. T!" Ollie said, following his brother back to the front of the submarine. As they settled behind their steering wheels, they observed the buttons more closely.

"I wonder what this one does," Ollie said, pointing to one.

"Don't touch that!" Joey snapped.

"Since when did pointing mean touching?" Ollie teased as he pointed rather closely at Joey's arm.

"Seriously! There's a lot of buttons here." Joey looked at each one. "How are we supposed to know which one to press?"

"Take a risk," Ollie said in a mocking tone. "Honestly, how do you even know we need to press any of these?" Ollie looked at Joey who was busy analyzing each of the buttons. The lights that were flashing around them were pressuring Joey to make a decision.

"I don't know. I just have a feeling we need to select one of these," Joey replied.

"Welp, this is stressing me out. I'm gonna go take a bath." Ollie rose from his seat.

"Ollie!" Joey yelled, stopping his brother in his tracks. "You seriously should be excited to get back into this! We can actually learn how to *control* our abilities! We haven't discussed any of our sixth senses in forever! I mean, aren't you the least bit excited?"

"You're right. I need to get over my fear of fear. I mean, we made it this far. So, let's go ahead and choose a button." Ollie sat back in his seat.

"Alright! Us driving this thing has to be a lot like Mom and Dad driving their cars, right? So, all we have to do is drive and figure out the best place to stop at," Joey said.

"Yeah, but we need to choose a button first — plus, we don't even know how to drive. I'm not trying to mess up or get lost like Aunt Olivia does when she drives." The boys laughed then stared harder at each of the buttons. "You know, I think deciding which button to push is your decision."

"Mine?"

"Yes," Ollie nodded.

"Why?" Joey questioned.

"Just like you have a feeling about things, so do I. So, it's just a feeling I have right now and I'm going to listen to my gut," Ollie replied. Joey kept staring intently at the buttons.

"Well, yellow means positivity, blue means wisdom —" Joey murmured.

"I don't know what you're saying, but if blue means wisdom, I must be blue," Ollie said proudly.

"OK, and purple means royalty, green means growth, red means passion, orange means friendliness, and…"

"What?" Ollie tried getting his brother's attention.

"Black. I don't know what black means. I haven't really figured that one out," Joey looked down at his feet.

"Well, if you're going to know the definitions for all the colors, you need to at least know the one that's literally our last name, Joey!" Just then, a loud beeping began. "What's happening?" Ollie cried.

"I think we seriously just need to pick a button!" Joey cried.

"I seriously think this is your decision!" Ollie crossed his arms and leaned back. Joey felt uneasy by the pressure, but he knew he had to take his own advice and take whatever consequence came with whichever button he pressed. The lights around them started blinking faster. The beeping was growing louder. Sweat began trickling down Joey's face as he extended his arm to press an orange button. After he did, the beeping stopped, the lights went back to a subtle blinking rhythm, and a chart appeared on the screen before them. It read, *Yellow is irresponsibility, Blue is fear, Purple is moodiness, Green is jealousy, Red is warning, Orange is ignorance, and Black is mystery.*

"These were not the definitions you were mumbling about," Ollie muttered.

"Yeah, guess not." Joey tore a sheet out from his notebook that he found sitting next to him. He quickly began scribbling the definitions down.

"Well, at least we know what our last name means," Ollie shrugged. Suddenly, their surroundings changed. Joey shoved the piece of paper into his pocket and watched Ollie's eyes grow wide. They had no idea how it happened, but they appeared to be inside of a car — Aunt Olivia's car, to be exact.

"Woah, how did we get in here?" Joey quickly looked at where they were sitting. The car was parked but they didn't know exactly where because they couldn't see out any of its windows. Joey dismissed the orange haze he saw around. "This car is a mess! Why does Aunt Olivia keep such a messy car?"

"I don't know, but when I grow up, my car won't be like this," Ollie nodded.

"I wonder what the point of us being inside here is."

"Maybe it's an escape room — like the one Dad took us to that one time!" Ollie exclaimed.

"You may be onto something — but seriously, look at all this mess! It's worse than usual!" Joey exclaimed. The boys rummaged through the magazines, empty coffee cups, empty coffee travel mugs, lipsticks, receipts, and a mountain of napkins.

"Woah, what's my watch doing here?" Ollie held up his watch to show Joey.

"Weird. My notebook appeared in the submarine just a second ago too! I think you should try pressing the buttons on it." Ollie did as his brother suggested, but the watch was unresponsive. He shook it, hoping that would create the fix he needed, but it did not. "Well, there has to be clues somewhere in this car!" Joey exclaimed.

"Clues for what though?" Ollie asked.

"To get out of here!" Joey cried. The boys decided to systematically organize all of Aunt Olivia's items the best way they could. They tried to clean all the mess they saw in the five-seat car they were inside of. When they were done organizing, they checked underneath the seats and car mats for the slightest hint on how to escape. They kept checking the cup holders, the glove compartment, and the sunglass holder, but could not find any sort of clue.

"Well, what now?" Ollie asked. Joey continued looking around them. He was now focusing on where he saw the color orange beaming. It was most vibrant on the passenger seat car mat below, and the center console. He took out the definitions of the colors he had stashed in his pocket and began studying them.

"Remember how that screen said orange means ignorance — but I said orange meant friendliess? Well, I think it could mean both. I think we're the ones who have to determine which vibe we're facing," Joey said slowly.

"Alright, you actually make sense for once," Ollie said. "But why are we talking about orange, in particular?"

"I mean, I know you can't see it, but there's orange in this car. At least you saw me press the orange button back in the submarine," Joey shrugged.

"Joey, all of the buttons in the submarine were white. This has definitely got to be all about you. I don't think I can help at all."

"Don't be the person who always says they can't be the one to help. We are meant to help one another, remember?" Joey replied. Ollie nodded and continued trying to turn his watch on.

"OK, so what made you choose the orange button instead of any of the other colors that I'm assuming you saw?"

"I...I...don't know, but I gotta deal with what comes with my choice, right? Oh, and just so you know, I see a lot of orange right there and right there." Joey pointed to the passenger seat's car mat and then to the center console. "So, I think our answer must be…" Joey reached down to flip the car mat over but ended up losing his balance and tumbling to the floor.

"Did you drop a beat again?" Ollie laughed. Joey ignored his brother and held up a green dog treat inside of a plastic bag.

"How did we not see this when we were cleaning?" Joey asked.

"I don't know, but it looks like the same dog treat Mr. Café gave you that day. Keep it in your pocket!" Joey nodded and shoved it into his pocket. He then looked inside the car's center console. He did so several times, but didn't find anything inside.

"Wait," Ollie said, re-opening the console and reaching his whole arm inside of it. Ollie suddenly lost his balance and completely fell through. Joey reached his arm down in the same manner, and fell through too. The boys found themselves in pitch darkness. They couldn't see one another, but knew they were standing next to one another.

"Ollie?" Joey whispered.

"Yeah?" Ollie whispered back.

"Where are we?"

"If I knew, I'd tell you," Ollie replied.

"Well, you're the wiser one!" Joey snapped.

"You're the older one — and *you* brought us here with your orange button obsession!"

"OK, let me think. What was both ignorant and friendly about any of that in the car?"

"I mean, it was nice and friendly of us to clean out her car for her," Ollie said.

"Yeah, alright — no. I don't think that's it. I think it was testing us more for our level of ignorance. Plus, I don't think that was really even her car. It was a replica," Joey replied.

"What's a replica?"

"Like a similar version of something, but not the real thing," Joey said.

"Oh, just like the government does with our food," Ollie sighed.

"Alright, so I think it was ignorant of us to think your watch couldn't help us piece something together back there that could have maybe — I don't know — started the car?" Joey said. "Do you still have your watch?"

"Yeah, it's in my hand — and I'm pressing buttons, but don't see anything lighting up. I hope I don't drop this thing. It's so dark in here!"

"OK, keep pressing, and we'll just make a mental note to be smarter next time."

"Well, how can there be a next time if we never get out of here?" Ollie cried.

"Relax. We're still debriefing what we did."

"What's debriefing mean?"

"I don't know. I hear Dad say that all the time," Joey replied.

"Stop saying words you don't know the meaning of."

"No! It makes me feel smart!"

"Whatever!"

"Keep pressing your watch's buttons, Ollie!"

"I am!"

"Great. Anyway, I think being in that car and seeing things for how they looked versus what they could be showed *our* ignorance," Joey proclaimed.

"OK, one question," Ollie said. "What is ignorance? Do you really even know?"

"Yes. It's like choosing to dismiss something rather than face the truth of it all. Many ignorant people accuse someone of something *they* do themselves," Joey replied.

"Oh, OK — like how you were complaining about Aunt Olivia's car being messy when your room is equally that way all the time." Just then the lights came on. Ollie's watch turned on, as well. Across the watch's screen read, *Search*.

"Woah," the boys said together as they looked around. They were inside of a home they did not recognize. The living room walls around them had a strip of floral wallpaper around its borders. There was a pale pink couch with a painting of an African woman hanging on the wall above. A red rug sprawled itself across the middle of the room, creating a divide between the couch and a vintage looking black loveseat that faced an even more vintage looking floor lamp and tall, skinny bookshelf in the far corner.

"Should we walk around here?" Ollie asked, slightly eager to do so.

"Yes, but...quietly. Somebody could be here," Joey said.

"Listen, I know how to be quiet. You're the loud one," Ollie snapped. The boys peeked around the corner where they found a heavily violet colored kitchen. The only other colors came from the white fridge, black stove, and yellow curtains. Near the bay window was a steaming plate of chocolate chip cookies.

"Take a cookie," Joey teased.

"My concern is not turning poor right now, Joseph," Ollie replied.

"OK, well, something tells me we aren't alone." Joey scanned the room.

"Well, you never are when someone says that line," Ollie replied. Joey shrugged then motioned for his brother to be quiet. He heard faint sounds coming from the other side of the house. The boys tip-toed toward the sound to find a man and woman sitting on a couch. Their backs were to them, but the boys could see what they were wearing. The man was in a suit while the woman was in a yellow dress with pearls around her neck and wrists. They were drinking coffee as they watched a program on a bulky looking television set.

"Why are they so dressed up?" Joey whispered. Ollie motioned for his brother to be quiet.

"Jackie Robinson is playing tonight," the woman said to the man.

"Good. Hurry home so we can enjoy watching the whole thing together," he replied. "I'm proud to have been following Robinson since his Quebec days."

"Yeah, I'll do my best to hurry home. I'm really just enjoying this new job. I mean, don't get me wrong, it's a lot of work, but it's serving a real purpose, you know? I mean, I do worry every time about the future." She took a large sip of coffee. "Like what happens when —"

"Please," the man interrupted. "Stop worrying and start believing. Worrying is a choice. Remaining calm and being happy is also a choice. So, you can choose to believe without being ignorant about things." He slowly sipped his coffee.

"My parents drink a lot of coffee, huh?" A little girl in a blue dress faced Ollie and Joey out of nowhere.

"Um...uh...hi," Joey whispered hesitantly while clearing his throat.

"You don't have to whisper. They can't hear you," she whispered.

"They can't?" Ollie questioned.

"Nope. I can though." She smiled and playfully began skipping. "I had a dream you were coming — and just so you know, I'm not afraid of any of this. It's nice to have friends. Mom doesn't let people come over. She's afraid of many things. She's afraid of people coming over and judging things. She's afraid we'll lose all of our money one day. She's probably even afraid that those cookies in the kitchen will get eaten by a random raccoon that comes into the house. She makes up a lot of things and begins worrying about them."

"Sorry, but we don't get any of this. We aren't even sure why we're here or where we are right now," Ollie replied.

"Oh, I don't know why either. I was just told to expect you. I may be five years old, but I'm a big girl who will never be afraid of anything ever!" She stood as tall as she could.

"So, what's your name?" Ollie asked.

"You can call me J.B.," the girl replied. "And I already know you are Oliver and you are Joseph. I'm the only child, but since the war's over now, I want to live freely and make new friends!" She went to the nearby window and looked out. "Mom promised I could once the war was over, but she still won't let me play outside unless she happens to already be out there watering the flowers — which she hardly does because she's always at work!" She stomped away from the window. "So, yeah, I just play with the new puppy my parents gave me." Just then, Sapphire walked in and licked J.B.'s ear. Sapphire then walked over to Joey, and sniffed his pocket. Joey pulled out the stashed treat he had, which Sapphire gobbled down in seconds.

"What are we doing here exactly?" Joey asked Sapphire as she licked her lips.

"What you need to," Sapphire replied, still licking her lips.

"Please, just help us!" Joey begged.

"Get to know the girl. That'll help you. I just stopped by to say hi and collect my treat you found from the last obstacle course. Oh, I also came to tell you to explore your animal instincts more. Just so you know, you don't always have to make animal noises to communicate with animals."

"What?" Joey had absolutely no idea what she was talking about. Sapphire began walking away, but then turned around to face Joey again.

"Oh, and have Ollie pay attention to his watch better please." After watching Sapphire dash out of sight, J.B. and Ollie stood still, looking at Joey with confusion.

"Why were you barking and whining like a puppy?" J.B. asked.

"Tell us! What did Sapphire say?" Ollie asked.

"Woah! Her name isn't Sapphire! Her name is Diamond!" J.B. protested.

"Yeah, maybe in another life," Ollie scoffed.

"She said she wants you to pay attention to your watch and that we need to get to know you more." Joey faced J.B.

"Oh, well, that won't be a problem. I have lots of toys. Do you want to play with my dolls or do you want to do my hair? I'm open to either," she replied.

"Neither," the boys said at the same time.

"Well, you guys are mean and I'm leaving!" J.B. stomped away.

"Wait!" Ollie called after her. "Please, just tell us where we are!"

"OK, sure! You're inside of my —" J.B. was interrupted by her mother's scream.

"Ah, I tore my dress!" she cried. The hem of her mother's dress was caught on the coffee table.

"How did that happen?" her father asked, setting his coffee cup down before offering his assistance.

"If I knew, I would tell you," the woman replied sharply. "Ugh, now I'm going to be late!"

"You have so many dresses, Alicia — just go in there and pick another one," the man replied.

"You realize the dresses I choose are done with great purpose, right? Each outfit I wear goes with a certain hairstyle. The shoes I climb into and the sweater I allow to hug my shoulders are meticulously planned. My fashion has never been a dash-and-go type of deal, Michael Joseph Broussard," she said as she unhooked her dress from the table's grasp and walked away.

"I understand that," he said as he reached for the cookie sitting in front of him. "But I'm rooting for you to find another contender back there!"

"Wow, my Mom would be so upset if she ripped her dress like that. She would have said how

everyone would be able to tell since it's yellow —
but I wonder if all rips are noticeable and it has
nothing to do with the color," Ollie looked toward
the ceiling as he pondered.

"Um, her dress was black," Joey replied.
J.B. and Ollie looked at Joey blankly. "Uh oh — it
wasn't? Well, I gotta figure this one out now." He
reached into his pocket to retrieve the crumpled up
color cheat sheet he had.

"What's he talking about?" J.B. whispered.

"Oh, he sees color," Ollie said nonchalantly
before redirecting his attention back to Joey.
"Remember black means mystery."

"Oh, yeah, and of course, black is the color I
haven't figured out the other meaning of!" Joey
threw his hands in the air.

"Well, I didn't know colors had meanings,
but my Mom has lots of colorful dresses. All I can
tell you is that my mother is one powerful woman in
the civil rights —" Just then, Ollie's watch began
beeping. It read, *BINGO* across its screen.

"Your watch must beep when we get
something right!" Joey replied, jumping with joy.

"I'm sure it can do more than just that. I just
haven't figured the rest of it out yet." Ollie
continued pressing various buttons on his watch.

"Well, it beeped after J.B. explained her
mother being a powerful woman. So, the other

meaning for the color black must be power!" Joey replied.

"OK, OK — you gotta tell us more about you." Ollie looked intently at J.B.

"Well, I don't do much. Like I said, I'm five, and you don't want to play with my toys so..."

"OK, then tell us about *when* we are," Joey replied.

"What do you mean by when?" she asked.

"What year?" Joey asked.

"Well, all I hear the grown ups keep saying is how it's still the Golden Radio Era, so I guess that's *when* it is. See, that thing on the wall even has radios all over it." She pointed at a calendar. The boys examined it closely and looked at the tiny font on it that read, *1947*. "And since it's summertime, I want a popsicle like every day — but Mom's afraid I'll choke on the stick it comes with, so we never buy any."

"Alright, well, there's several things I want to say about that, but we don't have that kind of time. Although, I will say, that is a sad way to live." Joey shook his head then began wandering around the room.

"Hey, so you look familiar." Ollie squinted his eyes at J.B.

"I do?" she questioned.

"Ollie time travels so you've probably met him before or something," Joey shrugged.

"Well, I don't know about that because I'm not allowed to travel," she said. "Mom thinks if I leave this house, I could get kidnapped!"

"OK, just relax and maybe teach us how to do your hair," Joey said, redirecting the conversation. J.B ran to get her hair ties, comb, and brush that was stored inside of a hatbox.

"Here, just use this and this, and put my hair up like that." She used her hands to demonstrate how she wanted her hair to be done. "So, you guys should tell me more about you." She held a floral hand mirror up to her face as she watched the boys attempt to earn their cosmetology licenses.

"Well, besides our abilities you now know about...um we're also brothers — but *I'm* the older one," Joey proclaimed.

"And I'm the wiser one," Ollie added.

"My grandpa used to say that to his brother," she laughed. "I remember both of them from all the way back from when I was four." The boys were huffing and puffing with exhaustion, but managed to place two hair buns at the top of her head. J.B. took a moment to examine her hair in the mirror. "Well, you did the best you could." She put her mirror and hair tools away before facing the boys. "So, you said the color black means both power and mystery, right? Well, that's interesting — but anyway, every week I listen to the radio with my parents." She walked them over to the kitchen where a large radio sat. "See, right here? This is where we listen to *The Jack Paar Radio Show*."

"Who? I mean, why?" Joey was at a loss for words.

"I mean, it's a comedy but —" she began.

"What?" Joey interrupted her.

"*The Jack Paar Radio Show*. Mr. Reaves from down the street said they are coming out with a kid's show called *Kukla, Fran and Ollie* for the tube!"

"Hey! That's me!" Ollie exclaimed.

"Oh, true!" she exclaimed. "So, is it your show? Do you play the 'Ollie' in it?"

"Oh, I...I don't think so," Ollie softly replied.

"Wait. What's the tube?" Joey asked.

"What?" J.B raised an eyebrow.

"You said that show is playing for some tube?" Joey questioned.

"Oh — sorry. Dad says we need to be sensitive to those who can't afford one, so I shouldn't have brought it up."

"No, no. We're not from this time period. We just need to understand the world you're living in so we can get out of here?" Joey replied.

"You wanna leave me? We were having so much fun," she whimpered.

"Don't take it personally," Joey replied.

"OK, well, I guess it's almost my bedtime anyway," she said, wiping her tears.

"So?" Joey asked.

"So?" J.B. replied.

"So, what's the tube?" Joey cried.

"Oh, it's the television," she whispered.

"You don't have to whisper, remember? You said your parents can't hear us," Ollie replied.

"They can't hear you, but they can hear me. I'm from here, remember?"

"OK, so we must be here to see if you are on that show?" Joey looked at Ollie intently.

"But it hasn't even aired yet!" Ollie protested. The boys began pacing the floor as J.B fixed her hair.

"We can always do my hair again to help you guys think better," J.B. suggested.

"No!" they both yelled. J.B. got up and began tuning the radio. The boys stopped pacing the floor and stood next to her. The radio signal was weak. All they could make out was laughter from the audience on a couple of stations. Just then, Sapphire walked back in and sat on top of something white and rectangular.

"What is this underneath Sapph — I mean Diamond?" Ollie asked as he pet her.

"It looks like a puzzle!" J.B exclaimed. The pieces were all dismantled. So, they worked quickly at putting it together. As they did, J.B.'s father warned her from afar that he was coming to tuck her into bed soon. Ollie, Joey, and J.B. worked even quicker. In the nick of time, the puzzle pieces were all in place. However, its picture remained blank. They all looked at Sapphire who only blinked at them in response.

"Joey, talk to her!" Ollie cried. Joey attempted to talk to Sapphire, but she quickly walked away.

"Let's run after Sapphire," J.B. said. As they ran, they were amazed they were not able to find her.

"I don't understand where she could have gone," Ollie said.

"Hey, J.B., you called her Sapphire! You said her name was Diamond." Joey squinted his eyes at J.B.

"Well, that name is now growing on me," she replied. The three laughed, but quickly began exchanging looks of confusion and defeat as they walked back over to where they had left the puzzle. As they approached it, they were shocked to see it was now glowing red.

"Are all of you seeing this?" Joey asked with his jaw almost to the floor.

"Why's it red now? What's red mean?" J.B. looked at Joey.

"It means passion," Joey said enthusiastically while looking at Ollie's watch for verification. "Or...warning!" Just then, a huge wind filled the room. Ollie and Joey quickly found themselves back in darkness. After a few moments of uncertainty, *Warning: Black Family In Danger* flashed before them in big, red letters. Then, the boys were thrown back into the seats of their submarine.

"Oh, you're back," Mr. Tender said calmly. The boys' legs were wobbly. Like honey to a biscuit, they wanted to stay stuck to their seats. They wanted time to sit and process all that had just occurred, but instead, they fought the urge and wobbled over to Mr. Tender. "I made you both different kinds of sandwiches. One of them is turkey. The other one is chicken." He placed the plates in front of them.

"Dude, did you get the turkey or the chicken?" Joey whispered. Ollie rolled his eyes and switched their plates.

"So, how are you?" Mr. Tender smiled as he gathered oranges to make juice. "You two have a lot more to do before you get back to your parents —

but tell me, how was it meeting your grandmother as a kid?" Suddenly, Joey saw black all around Mr. Tender, and Ollie's watch began beeping.

About the Author

Alyssa is a proud dog mom, daughter, sister, and supportive friend. She values caring for the planet and all the life in it. Alyssa has continually dedicated both her education and real world work to encouraging people to discover their true destiny. She was a recognized poet in grade school, an honors student in high school at Wildwood School, and earned her bachelor's degree from Chapman University's Dodge College of Film and Media Arts. She values learning from others and building ethical relationships from anyone she meets. Her long walks with Amber, agility course exercises with Jasper, and nature-watching sessions with Sapphire remind her to stay grounded and remain thankful. Life has led her to a café many times to help her truly color in the dreams of her
SIXTH SENSE.

ᦉ This book is part of the Ollie + Joey ® franchise. Collect the whole series and merchandise as you explore more of their world online!

198